DEATH - A CONSTANT COMPANION: ABUSE - A COINED DISASTER THAT KILLS THE SPIRIT

CeCe

DEATH - A CONSTANT COMPANION: ABUSE - A COINED DISASTER THAT KILLS THE SPIRIT

JR CONWAY

CITIOFBOOKS, INC.
3736 Eubank NE Suite A1
Albuquerque, NM 87111-3579
www.citiofbooks.com

Hotline: 1 (877) 389-2759
Fax: 1 (505) 930-7244

Ordering Information:
Quantity sales. Special discounts are available on quantity purchases by corporations, associations, and others. For details, contact the publisher at the address above.

Printed in the United States of America.

ISBN-13: Paperback   979-8-89391-466-5
          eBook   979-8-89391-467-2

Library of Congress Control Number: 2024924776

Chapter 1

Sweetwater, Texas is located along US Hwy 20, 125 miles southeast of Lubbock and 190 miles west of Ft Worth. Wind Farms and oil pumping stations are prominent throughout the surrounding area. It is also the county seat of Nolan County with a population a little over ten thousand.

Walt Ferguson moved to Sweetwater with his wife Stella when the wind industry found the area favorable to the placement of wind turbines. He found a job with an energy company headquartered there. It was on the job that he met Ken Parsons, a self-ordained minister of the Faith Ministry, a church he founded. Preacher Parsons believed that Men were the Chosen ones and women were created to serve them.

Walt and Stella had one child, a daughter they had named Bethea and called her Beth for short. The relationship between Stella and Walt was never warm, mostly because of his drinking, but after he had his family join the Faith Ministry, Stella and Beth were treated like servants and were subservient to Walt and the male members of the congregation.

Ken and his wife Terresa had two children, Daniel the oldest and Celine, nicknamed CeCe, the younger of the two. All females were required to wear long dresses that were hemmed at the ankles. No jeans or pedal pushers or shorts were permitted. Males however dressed in work type clothing or whatever was required by the companies they worked for.

Daniel was a handful for Terresa. Doctors told her early on that he might be autistic. He didn't conform to any type of guidance or discipline. His antics infuriated her, and she frequently beat him because she didn't comprehend or understand his condition and why he acted as he did. CeCe on the other hand was treated much nicer even though she was very close to her brother and had a calming influence on him.

Over time Faith Ministry had grown to the point that a school, not certified by the state of Texas, was established and all children of church members attended it. Much of the curriculum was domestic. The girls were educated in home economics, cooking, sewing and such. The boys were taught woodworking, mechanics, construction skills (Carpentry, framing, roofing and the preparation of concrete). Then there were the cult-like subjects, religious in nature, that were based on the beliefs of Ken Parsons. It was in the school that Beth, CeCe and Daniel had become friends.

One day as they were sitting on a bench eating lunch together, Daniel had blurted out that he was going to run away, that his mother would never be able to beat him again. Beth and CeCe thought he was just being Daniel and dismissed his outburst. Daniel began to explain what he was planning to do. He was going to go down to the train tracks and get on a slow-moving Freight. He said that he'd find an empty one of those cars that carry wire, or rock and stuff and hide until he was a long way from Sweetwater. The girls sat up, paying attention.

"If you run away Daniel, I'm going with you," CeCe said. "Why don't you come go with us?" She asked Beth.

Beth stopped chewing on an apple she had been eating. She had never thought of such a thing. The idea sounded adventurous to her.

"Okay!" When are we going?" Beth asked.

"Tonight," Daniel said. He was so excited that he was bouncing up and down on the bench.

"Be still Daniel," CeCe said. "How are we doing this?"

"When everybody is sleep," Daniel explained. "We sneak out and go down to the tracks and hide behind the station house. Trains go by real slow all night. We find an empty car and climb in. No body will see us. If you get there first Beth, wait for us. If we get there first we'll wait for you, OK?"

As planned the three met behind the station house. Beth had a small cooler with her.

"What's that?" Daniel asked.

"We're going to get hungry," Beth said. "So I got some pop, and some hot dogs, cheese sticks and some bread."

They were in luck. There was a train with a long line of box cars on a siding. There were two engines, and they were stopped a little ways past the station house where they were hiding. Daniel cautioned the girls to be quiet because in the lights that lite the area he could see some men standing near the first engine. They huddled together against the station house wall and waited for a long time. Then they heard the roar of the big motors start up on the engines and the train began to move very slowly. Daniel beckoned the girls to follow him, and they ran across several sets of tracks to the moving train.

As the box cars went by they saw that all the doors were closed and sealed. They became fearful that they would be caught. Fortunately, the engines were out of sight now and they couldn't be seen by the men on board them. The box cars kept coming by and they were all locked. Beth looked down the track and saw that there was still a lot of the train to come. She grabbed Daniel by his shoulder and whispered to him.

"Look Daniel. There comes some that have cars in them. They're open on the end." Daniel began jumping up and down in his excitement.

"Be still Daniel," CeCe said. "Somebody might see us." As one of the car carriers approached they began trotting alongside at the same speed. There was a step at the very end of the carrier and Daniel helped CeCe up, then Beth handed CeCe the cooler and climbed up,

Daniel boarded last. There wasn't much room between the cars and the side of the carrier, but they could sit comfortably if they stuck their legs under the cars.

Once outside the populated area of Sweetwater, the train began to pick up speed and Daniel began to giggle. "No more beatings," he kept saying in a singsong fashion. Beth and CeCe huddled close together as the increased speed of the train caused the cool night air to flow through the carrier and they had not dressed for it. Their long dresses gave no protection against the chill of the night air.

The train passed through Lubbock and Amarillo the first two days, and Pueblo, Colorado and Denver the next two days. After the fourth day and night, the conditions were such that the girls could no longer bear the discomfort. The food had been long gone CeCe began to cry a lot and Beth kept pestering Daniel that they should go back, that running away was a bad idea. Daniel was not having it. He kept saying that he would not go back and if they didn't stop crying and fussing he would beat them.

"How far do you want to go?" Beth asked

"Far enough that they will never find us." Daniel said.

"Aren't you hungry?" Beth asked. "I'm so hungry I feel like I'm going to be sick, and CeCe can't take any more of this. We need to get off."

"NO! No! no! no!" Daniel screamed. "Shut up; maybe we'll get off tonight. I don't know, maybe."

"Daniel!" Beth was frantic. "The next time this train slows down, I'm taking CeCe and we're getting off. You do what you want."

True to her word when the train slowed down again Beth and CeCe got off. Both called to Daniel to get off, CeCe even ran alongside the train begging him to get off, but he ignored her cries, and she had to give up. She sat along the tracks in the dirt and cried. Beth sat beside her and tried to comfort her. When they stood up they could see cars and trucks moving on a highway. There were some parked at a building also. It was a short distance through some tumble weeds to the highway. They decided to walk to the building. Maybe they could find something to eat there.

The building happened to be a rest stop on Interstate 80 and that's where Katie found them-afraid, despondent, dirty and hungry. Without giving it much thought, after seeing the desperate situation the girls were in, Katie decided to take them with her to the home of her parents, Craig and Martha Spence.

By the time Katie arrived with the girls, Craig had hamburgers on a platter that he placed on the kitchen table. Martha greeted each of the girls with a big hug and guided them to chairs at the table. Without a word being said, CeCe grabbed a burger and Beth looked longingly at Martha.

"Go on, go for it," Martha said to Beth. Craig, Martha and Katie just stood silently by and watched the girls devour those burgers. Martha brought a large plastic bottle of Orange Aid from the fridge and kept glasses full for them. To Katie she said, "I'm so glad you did this. These babies are in bad shape. Go to the linen closet in our bed room and get some quilts and blankets that are stacked on the floor. Bring them out and spread them over behind the couch."

When Martha turned to look at the girls, CeCe was holding a half-eaten burger in her hand and her head was bowed and cocked to one side, she was asleep. Martha took the burger and CeCe jerked awake.

"Okay, young lady, I think you've eaten enough for now come with me and let's see if we can get some of that road filth off you." Martha leaned close to CeCe and whispered. "I think you'll smell better too." CeCe managed a small smile and went off with Martha.

Craig poured more Orange Aid in Beths glass and pulled up a chair next to her. For the first time he took note of the way she was dressed. He recalled that when he was Sheriff he had seen people belonging to religious groups pass through the county dressed like that. He spoke to her.

"How long have you been on the go," he asked.

"I think we were on the train four, maybe five days, sir."

"You didn't eat for five days? That's hard to believe. No wonder you two stuffed those burgers down," Craig said in wonder.

"We had hot dogs the first two or three days, but they didn't last long," Beth related.

"Was to run away your idea," Craig asked.

"No sir," Beth said between bites of her third burger. "It was CeCe's brothers idea."

"Katie only picked up you and the other girl. Where's the boy?" Craig asked with some concern in his voice.

" He wouldn't come. He stayed on the train."

"Why don't you tell me why all of this happened," Craig said. Beth relaxed in her chair and began with her family life, the church school, all about the way women and girls were treated. She told Craig about Daniel maybe being Autistic. and why he had decided to run away.

"When Daniel told us he was planning to run away", Beth continued. "CeCe and I decided to go with him."

Martha returned with CeCe who was dressed in one of Martha's PJ tops. It was much too big, but it would do. Now that her hair was clean the red really stood out.

"Ok young lady," Martha said to Beth. "it's your turn." Beth went off with Martha and CeCe slid into the chair where she had sat. Craig with a big hand ruffled her red hair and with a big smile on his face commented on her appearance.

"You clean up pretty good young'un," he said. "Why don't you scoot over to them blankets and get some sleep. Come on, I'll tuck you in." As he covered her CeCe began to cry.

"What's wrong little lady," he asked.

"Daniel," she said as the tears rolled down her cheeks. "He's out there all alone somewhere. I wish he were here."

"Don't fret baby girl," Craig said as he again ruffled her red hair. "In the morning we'll try and find him." A hand was ruffling his hair. It was Katie. She was kneeling on the couch watching him over its back. When he looked up at her she said nothing, but she had a proud of you daddy smile on her face.

The day started for Stella as usual, standing on the front porch of their modest home, cup of coffee in hand, watching the sun come up. Every morning, before anyone began to stir she made a pot of coffee and watched the sun come up out of the plains, way out in the distance. The morning air was so cool and fresh, it made her feel good. She'd stand there holding the coffee cup in both hands until she'd hear Walt stumbling around getting ready for work. She'd then return to the kitchen and prepare breakfast. Once Walt was off to work she'd wake Beth, and they would share breakfast before Beth was off to school.

Stella stood frozen, squeezing the door knob on the door as she stared into Beths room. The bed had not been slept in. Had she forgotten that Beth was going to spend the night at CeCe's house? No, she thought. They hadn't talked about it. Where is she, what has happened to her? Stella stepped into the room searching for some clue. Beths cloths hung neatly in a cubby hole in the wall. There was no closet. Her shoes were gone and only the dress that Beth wore the day before was missing.

Stella hurried to the phone that sat on a small table in the hallway between the master bedroom and the room that was Beths. She dialed Terresa's number. The phone rang and rang. Stella became more anxious as she waited. Why doesn't Terresa answer, she thought. Finally, after what seemed to be a very long time Terresa answered. Stella's name showed on the caller ID.

"Hello Stella," she said. Her voice high pitched. "Have you seen Daniel and CeCe? Their beds aint been slept in. They're not here."

"O my God Teressa," Stella said almost in a whisper. "I was calling to see if maybe Beth was over there. Her bed aint been slept in either. What's going on?" Stella could tell that Teressa was crying. Teressa was scared and so was she, but she had to keep herself together.

"Have you said anything to Ken?" Stella asked.

"No," Teressa replied. "He's gonna holler at me when he finds out."

"You call and let him know and I'll get ahold of Walt and see if we can figure this out," Stella tried to sound calm. She hung up the phone and went back to Beths room to take one more look before she called Walt.

Beth had a teddy bear that she always kept against her pillow when her bed was made. Stella hadn't noticed before, but it's arms were positioned so that it cupped it's little paws and it was holding a slip of paper. She could feel her heart beating in her chest as she took the paper from the bear. It was a note. It just said, "LOVE YOU MOM."

CHAPTER 2

Steve Lolly had carried on the tradition of morning briefings that had worked so well through the Craig Spence years and the years of his predecessor Harry Kushner. Over the last couple of years he had been able to increase the size of the department to include a new jail administrator, a new chief of detectives, two additional investigators and six additional patrol deputies.

The jail administrator, Tera Mosby, had been in charge of the Sheridan County jail for a number of years and felt she needed to make a change in her life when she applied for the job in Sweetwater County. She had raised a son and daughter who now had families of their own. She had been living alone since her husband had had a midlife crises and moved on with a younger woman. Tera was a tall woman but couldn't have topped ninety pounds. She was skinny. A person with normal sized hands could wrapped them around her thighs and the fingers and thumbs would meet. She wore her dark hair pulled up on top of her head and tied there, causing the ends to flow over like a fountain. Her eyes were large with pupils jet black, very pronounced in the light skin of her face.

The man who replaced Kevin as the head of the detectives, George Stenson, was older than most of the departments personnel. He had been an investigator with the US Postal Service for twenty-three years, retired and moved from Virginia to Wyoming with his wife to enjoy the outdoors, hunting and fishing. While the two of them were on a fishing trip in the Jackson Hole area his wife had an aneurysm and passed away. After a year or two of being alone he began to look around for something to keep him busy. When the job at the Sheriff's Department came open he applied and was accepted.

George was short and chunky, not fat, but stubby with a broad torso, short arms and legs. He was bald through the middle of his head and salt and pepper hair along the sides that he kept cut very short. He had bushy eyebrows and wore a broad well-trimmed mustache that was almost white. He was always the first to arrive for meetings and this morning he was in the conference room when Steve got there.

"Good morning George," Steve said. "You spend the night here?" George chuckled.

"No, No," he responded. "Just believe in getting where I'm going early."

"Done any fishing lately," Steve asked.

"No, still a little too cold and windy," George replied. "The old bones don't handle the cold like they used to."

"I haven't taken my boat out for a couple of years," Steve continued. "I'll have to clean it up and maybe take you and Sherrif Spence out one of these days."

"Sounds good," George said enthusiastically. "Let me know when and I'll help you get it ready." As he made his offer Kevin entered the room.

"Good morning you two," he said as he covered his mouth to yawn.

"Late night huh?" Steve joked.

"Actually yes," Kevin said. "I'll let George tell you about it." Tera came through the door to the conference room moving in a hurry. She always moved as if she was going to a fire.

Steve opened the briefing by commending everyone for the way they were running their departments and complimenting them for the efficiency and effectiveness. Then he started getting the staff reports and started with Tera.

"What's happening in your area Ms. Mosby," he asked.

"Good Morning Sheriff," She started. "I don't think I've seen the jail with so few occupants since I came here. We only have one going to court this morning and we have six who are serving ninety-day sentences and three serving thirty- day. I'm using this lag time to get the cell walls and floors cleaned up."

"Enjoy it while you can," Kevin interjected. "There's a full moon next week."

"Does have a tendency to get crazy during the full moon," Steve commented. "I was browsing through last night's reports this morning and noticed one from Deputy Parker regarding an accidental death over in the Red Feather area west of town. What's that all about Kevin," Steve asked.

"About nine thirty last night dispatch got a call regarding a man down in his home," Kevin began. "The call was made by his wife. Parker was given the call and when he arrived he was let in by a woman who said she was Mrs. Paty Thorton, and she said that her husband had fallen down the stairs and he looks terrible.

The house is a tri level custom home with a stair case going from the second level to the third. The stair case begins with six steps, has a landing and changes direction with another ten steps. There was a latticed banister that closed of the stair case. The stairs were uncovered hard wood. A male person was found on the landing, head pressed against the wall across from the second set of stairs, lying on his stomach . According to Parker there was no doubt that the man's neck was broken because the head was at an odd angel from the body. Parker called for the paramedics and called me. When I got there the paramedics had already determined that the man, Dr Paul Thorton a local dentist, was dead. I called George here to come process the scene."

"You want to pick up from there George," Steve inquired.

"Yes sir," George began. "When I got there the body had been moved by the paramedics, but Parker had been smart enough to use a camera he carried in his patrol car to take pictures of the body as he found it. I took pictures of the way the deceased was dressed. He was dressed in a blue dress shirt, opened at the collar and a pair of light tan slacks. He was in his stocking feet and there were no shoes in the area. I took pictures of marks I could see on the body. There were marks along the left cheek, just below the left eye, a big bruise on the forehead and a bruise of the back of the right-hand. I took pictures of the layout of the place, outlined the body as it lay with chalk and then interviewed Mrs. Thorton. She might have been in shock because she was very quiet, I could hardly get her to answer my questions. I asked her if she wanted to call her doctor or a clergy or someone to be with her, but she answered in the negative. I also asked her if there was someplace she could spend a couple of days away from her home until the investigation of the incident could be concluded. She stated that she could spend a couple of days at her office in Rock Springs. I got the phone number of her business and advised her that I'd like to talk with her again in the next day or two. After some minutes she seemed to soften up a bit and I was able to get some information from her. I asked if she had any idea what happened. She replied that she was in the sitting room on the second level watching "The Price is Right" on the TV when she heard this awful noise on the stairs. When she went to look she found her husband lying on the landing. She started to tighten up at this point and for the first time I saw a little emotion."

"Is this cut and dried or does it require additional investigation?" Steve asked.

" I'll wait for the coroner's report to decide that" George replied.

Steve made notes on a pad that he had before him and then turned to Kevin, his next in command and patrol supervisor.

"How's things in your area Kevin?" He asked.

"We've had a rash of absentees on our patrol force due to a twenty-four-hour stomach flu that swept through," Kevin related. For the last few days we've been running skeleton operations. Hopefully, we'll back to normal in short order. I've nothing unusual or of any importance to report."

"Ok," Steve began. Things are pretty quiet in the county right now. The only thing that we might want to keep our ears open for is a movement by the cities of Rock Springs and Green River, along with the county, to establish a metropolitan type Board of Commissioners to oversee police operations throughout the county. Could be interesting. George, keep me tuned in to that Thorton situation. Let's go to work...."

Paul Thorton had practiced dentistry in Sweetwater County for several years and his wife ran a Massage Therapy business in Rock Springs. Paul worked at his office every week Tuesday through Thursday. He had a staff consisting of an office manager, a Registered Dental assistant, a Certified Dental assistant and a Dental Hygienist.

Once a month Paul traveled to Bellevue, Nebraska where his eighty-year-old mother lived alone in the family home, a four-bedroom two story structure that sat on twenty acres of land. Paul would spend a weekend making sure his Mom's car was in good condition, she still drove to the grocery store, doctor appointments and to church every Sunday; made sure her meds were properly sorted for each day; catching up on general care taker chores and arranging for any major repairs that were required.

On the weekend prior to his death, Paul went to Bellevue and his return trip was delayed because of blizzard conditions that had sweep through the area. He had notified his office and Paty that road conditions were horrible, and he would not be leaving until Wednesday instead of Monday as usual.

On Tuesday, when Paty broke for lunch, she decided to check in with Paul to see how the weather was and if he would be heading home as planned. She called his mother's phone number from her office. The phone rang several times and just as Paty was about to hang up Paul's mother answered.

"Hi Paty, how nice to hear from you," she said.

"How did you know it was me, Mama Preston?' Paty asked. Preston was Paul Thorton's mother's married name from a second marriage.

"Oh, Paul got me a phone with caller ID so I can see who's calling," Mrs. Preston replied with some glee. "That way I can see if I want to talk to whoever is calling."

"Great idea, Mama. How are you?" Paty asked.

"Oh, I'm alright. If I didn't have to put up with Arthur, life would be perfect," was her answer.

"Arthur?" Paty asked. Who's Arthur, Mama?"

"Arthritis dear. It comes with old age." She chuckled and Paty laughed with her.

"I'm glad you're doing well Mama Preston," Paty said. "May I talk to Paul?"

"Oh he's not here dear. He left yesterday morning," she said. "He should be home by now," she stated.

"I thought you were having bad weather there," Paty questioned.

"Oh yes," Mrs. Preston said. "It was awful, the wind blew and when I looked out the window the snow was going sideways, and you could hardly see. It stopped sometime Sunday night, then it cleared up. We've had sunshine since."

Paty didn't pursue the matter any further with Mrs. Preston, but she was confused. If the weather was no longer a problem, and he had left on Monday, why wasn't he home already. After hanging up with Mrs. Preston, the rest of Paty's day was a mass of questions. Where was he? What has happened? Has he had an accident? Why hasn't he called?....

When Steve got back to his office the button on the phone was blinking. That button indicated that Heather, his office assistant and secretary, wanted him to call her. He picked up the receiver, punched the button and heather came on.

"What's up Heather?" Steve asked.

"Sir, Sheriff Spence wants you to call him ASAP," she said. "He says he needs your help".

"Thanks," Steve said. "I'll call him straight away." After hanging up he used the speed dial to call Craig. Martha answered the phone.

" Hello," she said.

"Hey Martha," he responded. "This is Steve, how yall doing?

"We're fine Steve, haven't seen much of you recently. Are things okay with you," she asked.

"Doing fine," he replied. "Mertle and I spent a week in Laramie with Marla, attended orientation activities at the University. A couple of weeks before that we spent a week with Milly up at Yellow Stone National Park where she has been accepted for a job with the Department of Interior."

"My how wonderful," Marhta marveled. "When does Milly start her new job? No wonder Mertle hasn't been around. It's so nice that you two are spending time together."

"In a couple of weeks Milly is off to the Park," Steve answered. "She's busy getting her things together and we have also been out car shopping for her. She took her driver's test last week and passed so she's all excited."

"Well, I hope both of the girls will stop by and visit with us before they scoot off on their own," Martha said.

"I'm sure they will," Steve assured. "I have a message to call Sheriff Spence, is he around?"

"Yes Steve, he's watching a basketball game with his eye's closed, hang on," Martha said. She wasn't gone long before he heard Craig's voice.

"Hi, ya Steve, how you be," Craig inquired.

"I'm good, boss, you still doing ok?" Steve asked.

"Still keeping busy with my post cards," Craig replied. "Now that we're on the back side of winter, and scenery is changing again I'm out n about taking pictures whenever the weather is decent."

"You left a message for me to call you, what's up?" Steve asked.

"Yeh, Steve," Craig started. "I know it's early and you probably haven't planned out your day yet, but could we have lunch today? We've become involved in a situation that's going to take someone in your position to handle."

"Sure, your place or someplace else?" Asked Steve.

"How about up at the Pizza Hut? I haven't had pizza in a dog's age. You think we can meet there?" Craig suggested.

"Good idea," Steve said. Let's meet about eleven so we beat the crowd."

"I'll see you there. Thanks Steve," Craig agreed.

When Craig arrived at the Pizza Hut, Steve was already there and had taken a table in a far corner where they wouldn't be disturbed by people moving in and out. Craig slid in a seat across the table and began to relate the story of Katie bringing home the runaways and how Martha had cleaned them up and so on. Then he got to the part where he needed Steve's help.

"The two girls, Beth and CeCe are going to be fine," Craig continued. "I'll be calling Child Protective Services today and see what they can do to take care of them until their parents can be reached and a determination be made about their future wellbeing.

The problem is, there was a boy with them when they ran away. He's CeCe's brother. When the girls left the train he refused to come with them and the last they saw of him he was still on it. None of these kids were dressed for these cool nights and he hadn't eaten for a couple of days. We need to find this kid. I thought maybe if you were to call the railroad people you'd get a better reaction from them than I would if I called."

"Gees, boss!" Steve quietly exclaimed. "Do you know how many freight trains go through Sweetwater County every couple of days?"

"Will you do it," Craig asked.

"Of course I will," Steve replied. "Where are the girls now?"

"Katie rented a suite over at the Ramada and is staying with them there until we can get things moving," Craig advised.

"I'd better get on it," Steve said as he slid out of the booth. "The weather is forecasted to make a dramatic change in the coming days. Let's get together for dinner someday soon boss."

"Deal. Keep me posted will ya," Craig requested as they walked out of the building.

According to Wyoming law, everyone must report suspected abuse, neglect, or vulnerability of children or adults if they reasonably believe either of the above situations exist. The Department of Family Services then has twenty-Four hours to initiate an investigation. Such reports are investigated by the Child Protective Services Division.

The phone rang for so many times it was irritating. Craig held the receiver away from his ear so that Martha could hear the ringing.

"It's only nine in the morning," Martha commented. "Most public offices hold their daily or weekly meetings about this time".

"Most public services that are customer oriented have someone available to answer calls," Craig retorted. Finaly the ringing stopped and there was a clicking sound as if someone had picked up. A recorded voice began.

"You have reached the offices of the Wyoming Department of Family services. Our normal operating hours are between nine thirty and four thirty, Monday through Friday. You may leave a phone number where you can be reached and a short message regarding the reason for your call and a crises counselor will contact you, or you may try your call again during normal operating hours. Have a good day."

"Guess they have bankers hours up there," Craig said as he hung up the phone not hiding his irritation. "They don't even start working until nine thirty."

"So have another cup of coffee and give them time to open up," Martha suggested.

At nine forty- five, Craig called the Department of Family services again, and again he got a recording.

"You have reached the offices of the Wyoming Department of Family Services. All of our counselors are busy servicing other clients and customers. Please hold and your call will be answered in the order it was received"

The elevator music that followed didn't help Craig's disposition much, but he refrained from making any disparaging comments. After a short time the recorded voice returned.

"Please continue to hold. your call is important to us. A counselor will be with you momentarily."

Sure enough a very pleasant voice of a female human broke into the elevator music and Craig perked up.

"Good Morning," came the greeting. "My name is Carolyn; I apologize for your wait. May I ask to whom I'm speaking?"

"Carolyn, my name is Craig Spence, retired Sheriff of Sweetwater County," Craig replied.

"Ah yes," Carolyn said. "I never met you sir, but I had the pleasure of working with your office several years back in the case of an abandoned little girl that was a deaf-mute."

"I remember that case," Craig recalled. "What ever happened to her?"

"That was one case that I'm very proud of its resolution. That little girl was eventually placed with a married couple that was deaf and it was the most rewarding placement I've ever made. But what can I do for you, sir?"

"My daughter rounded up a couple of runaways a couple of days ago and they need to be cared for."

"What do you mean, they were rounded up?" Carolyn asked.

"They were cold and hungry, hiding at a rest stop along highway I-80," Craig related. My daughter happened to stop there and found them hiding in one of the stalls. Being the type person she is, she couldn't just leave them there, so she brought them home."

"What are their gender, " Carolyn asked.

"Two girls, ages twelve and fourteen, Craig replied. "They hopped a freight train in Sweetwater, TX. And jumped off here in Sweetwater County. There was a boy with them, but he stayed on the train. The sheriff here is making inquiries with the railroad people about him."

"Where are these children now?" Carolyn asked.

"My daughter has them in a suite at the Ramada Inn," Craig replied.

" As you are probably aware Mr. Spence," Carolyn began. "The Department of Family Services is a bureaucracy, and your acts of kindness may have complicated things a bit. From what you tell me these youngsters are not currently in any danger so those elements in the law which would facilitate urgent action don't apply. However, we do have to be concerned for their future welfare. So, I recommend that they be taken into custody by a law enforcement agency and the reporting process be started there. So I'll need to have a description of each girl and where they're located, and I'll initiate the request for them to be taken into custody by the appropriate enforcement agency."

Craig spent several moments providing Carolyn the physical descriptions of Beth and CeCe and relating to her what the girls had told him about their lives back in Sweetwater, TX., the condition the girls were in when they arrived and what Martha and Katie had done to care for them. He then called Katie at the hotel and explained to her what was going to take place.

Shortly after noon, Katie walked into the dining room at the Manor and made her way to the table where Craig and Martha were seated with Mertle. She retrieved a chair from a nearby table and sat heavily. She didn't say anything immediately but stuck her bottom lip out in a pout and laid her head on her mother's shoulder.

"Tell me what happened," Martha said placing her cheek on Katies forehead. Katie sat up and began to speak softly.

"I told the girls what dad had told me was going to happen and why," Katie began. "At first they were very apprehensive because they thought they were being punished. I explained to them that they couldn't stay with us for long because we would be breaking the law if we did. I explained to Beth that this would be the beginning of her getting help with her family situation and CeCe that she would be able to get help going back home if she wished. CeCe began to cry because she didn't know where her brother was, and she felt that her parents might blame her for leaving him. I couldn't answer all the questions they asked me, and I felt so useless. I think I finally convinced them that everything that was being done was for their good."

"Where are they now" Mertle asked.

"A female plain clothed police officer showed up. She identified herself as a Juvenile Detective with the Green River Police Department. She was very nice. She sat on the floor in front of the girls and explained to them what was happening, and she answered the questions that I couldn't. She told them that they were not going to jail, that they were going to be staying in a room at the hospital and someone would be watching over them night and day until Child Protective Service comes and talks to them. She explained who Child Protective Service were and what their job was. I think they really trusted her because they seemed to be more comfortable with the situation. I just wish they didn't have to go through this. I was beginning to wish I could keep them." She began pouting again.

CHAPTER 3

On Wednesday morning- George, the detective at the sheriff's office, received a call from the Coroner's office that the examination of Dr. Thorton's body had been completed and that he was welcome to come over for a briefing of the findings. When George arrived he was escorted into the morgue where the body was being kept in the cooler. Dr. Perkins, the county Medical Examiner, had his assistants place the body on a table under a bright light.

Dr. Perkins was a small man, wore granny glasses and his hair, long and unkept, hung down over his right eye. He began to speak into a microphone that was attached to the collar of his white coat. His voice was high pitched and sort of squeaky, George thought.

"This is Dr. Perkins, Sweetwater County Medical Examiner, and the time is ten -fifteen am on Thursday September eight, 1996. This is a briefing for the benefit of the Sweetwater County sheriff Departments investigator, Mr. George Stenson, regarding the case of Dr. Paul Thorton, the deceased. During my examination of the deceased it was determined that the cause of death was a fall which occurred in the home of the deceased on Wednesday September seventh, 1996, approximately between seven and nine pm. According to reports received the deceased fell down a flight of stairs. Examination revealed that the deceased suffered a cervical fracture resulting in a serious spinal cord injury and death." Dr. Perkins stopped talking and removed the sheet that covered the body. The body was lying on its back and Dr. Perkins pointed to the scratch marks on the right cheek below the right eye.

"These scratches are consistent with those made by finger nails." He explained and then rolled the body over onto its right side and continued speaking.

"Examination revealed several areas of Ecchymosis or bruises at spinal lumbar L1, L3, and L5. There were no bruises located on the stomach or chest areas. This indicates that the deceased fell backwards down the stairs." Dr. Perkins then rolled the body on to its back again and picked up the right arm. *"There is also an abrasion on the back of the right hand in which I found flakes of a brown lacquer. This also supports the hypothesis that the deceased was falling backwards and struck a painted object with the right hand. Examination of the decedents brain shows that he suffered a severe concussion."* Dr. Perkins looked up at George and asked. "Do you have any questions of me detective?"

"Yes Doctor," George began. "Dr. Thorton was in his stocking feet. Is it possible that he slipped on the hardwood floor?"

"Of course that is possible," the doctor surmised. *But had that been the case, I would expect to have found scrapes and bruising on the legs, especially on the calf's and buttocks."*

" I have no further questions sir," George said.

"This concludes this briefing at eleven -thirty am Thursday September eight, 1996," Dr. Perkins closed the briefing.

Back in his unmarked unit, George went over the notes he had been taking during the briefing. 1) The coroner estimated that the death occurred between seven and nine. 2) Dr. Thorton fell down the stairs backwards. 3) The scratches on his face are consistent with being made by finger nails. 4) The absence of bruising on the legs and buttocks would make slipping in his stocking feet unlikely.

When George arrived back at the Sheriff's Department, he went straight to the dispatching radio room and checked the logs for Wednesday night. He was able to confirm that the call came in at nine-thirty pm. That triggered the question, *what was happening from the time the fall was discovered, and the call being placed?* Something else caught Georges eye. The area code for Wyoming is three- zero-seven. The call reporting the accident came from area code five-zero-two. George retrieved a phone book from one of the dispatchers and found that area code five-zero-two was in Kentucky. The dispatchers log showed that the person reporting the incident was Mrs. Thorton and the contact phone number was five-zero-two, seven- seven-four, two-two-four-three.

George went to his office and placed a call to the number he'd found on the log. The phone rang seven times, George counted. Then a recorded voice of a woman came on.

"You've reached Sharon Thorton, I'm either busy or not available. Leave a message."

"Mrs. Thorton, this is Detective Stenson with the Sweetwater County Sheriff's Office," George said. "When you get this message please give me a call." George left his office phone number. He then placed a call to Mrs. Paty Thorton, the wife of Dr. Paul Thorton, and made an appointment for her to come to his office at three o-clock that afternoon. He had questions that only she could answer he told her.

Stella Ferguson cried most of the past week that Beth was gone. She now had begun to assimilate why her daughter would leave her home, and she accepted some of the blame. All of her life Beth had been treated like a servant. She was constantly being scolded or physically abused and she had stood by and let it happen. She had done all she could in an effort to find Beth. She had reported her missing to the Sweetwater Police Department the day she had found the note on her bear. They told her that they had to wait twenty- four hours before they would do anything. Walt, her husband was no help at all. As far as he was concerned it was good riddance. All he wanted to do was come home from work, his supper better be ready; sit in front of the TV and drink beer.

Terresa Parsons was a mess. Most of the time when she and Stella would talk about the kids, Terresa would get hysterical. Ken, her husband, was furious with them for running away. They had embarrassed him in the eyes of his church members. He kept saying that God would punish them severely. He wouldn't even ask the congregation to pray for their safety. It was so awful, Stella thought.

Stella was sitting in her kitchen close to the phone, hoping that someone would call and give her news about Beth and the other kids, not in a funk anymore but angry. She was angry at herself for not protecting Beth, for not being a more loving and stronger mother. She was angry at Walt for the way he treated her, and Beth, and she was angry at him for being sucked into that religious group that treated women and children so poorly. It was while she was sitting there that there was a knock at the door. When she opened it there was a man in a policeman's uniform. He was fat, his jacket was open and his shirt with the badge pined to it hardly buttoned over his protruding belly. Apparently he was a snuff or tobacco chewer because there was a stain out the corner of his mouth. Sure enough when he spoke there was something brown stuck to his teeth.

"Good Morning Ma'am," he began. "I'm officer Kennesy and I'm looking for Mrs. Uh, Mrs." –He paused and took a small note book out of the breast pocket of his shirt. "Oh yeh, Mrs. Stella Ferguson."

"That's me," Stella responded.

" You missing a child, Ma'am?" He asked.

"Yes officer, my daughter is missing. Do you have news?" Stella's heart was in her throat, and it was beating like a drum.

"What's your daughter's name Ma'am?" Kennesy asked.

"Beth! What is it?" Stella exclaimed, not able to stand the tension any more.

"Seems like she took quite a trip Ma'am," Kennesy said. "We got a call from an agency in Sweetwater County, Wyoming this morning and they said Beth is in custody there. They want you to call this number," Officer Kennesy handed Stella a piece of paper with a phone number on it.

"Oh thank you, thank you officer," Beth said , reaching out to shake his hand.

"Good day Ma'am and good luck," the officer said as he turned and returned to his car parked at the curb.

Stella just couldn't stop the tears from welling up in her eyes as she dialed the number. The phone on the other end rang and it was taking so long for someone to answer, she thought. Finally there was a clicking sound and a voice.

"you have reached the offices of the Wyoming Department of Family Services. Our counselors are currently busy servicing other clients and customers. Your call is important to us, please---" there was a break, and another voice spoke.

"This is the office of Wyoming Child Protective Services, my name is Carolyn, how may I help you?"

"I'm Stella Ferguson in Sweetwater, TX," She blurted out. "I was told to call this number about my daughter. Bethea, her name is Bethea, but we call her Beth," Stella said. "Do you have her?"

"Mrs. Ferguson, the only thing I can tell you is your daughter is safe and in good hands. You should be hearing from the Texas Health and Human Services Department, specifically the Department of Family Protective services in short order regarding Beth's future wellbeing."

"Ok, is she there? Can I talk to her? Stella asked.

"I'm sorry Ma'am, Beth is fine and that's all I can tell you. Any further information will have to come from the Texas Department of Family Protective Services. I hope knowing Beth is safe is comforting to you. Have a nice day."

"Yes, yes. Thank you very much," Stella said. There was a click and a dial tone. Carolyn had hung up. Stella sat for a long time and this time the tears were resulting from a feeling of happiness, the release of so much tension that had built up over the last few days. She dialed Teresa's Number.

"Teresa have you heard?" Stella said when Teresa answered.

"Oh yes , Stella," She responded. "But only CeCe. They don't know where Daniel is. He's still out there somewhere," she said as she began to cry again. This time they cried together as the tension that had built up over the past few days was released.

Stella was on the porch when Walt parked his pickup in the drive way. He walked toward the house with a small cooler that he carried his lunch in and a six pack of beer. Stella stood, arms folded over her chest, and her feet firmly planted. She was only five foot four and probably one hundred ten pounds, but she felt larger than ever before, and when she was upset her eyes turned from grey to green. They were green now. Walt was about to walk past her when she spoke.

"They found Beth," she said. Her words were matter of fact, without emotion. Walt stopped and turned to face her.

" So," he said. "Is she living or dead?"

"She's alive," Stella replied.

"Where'd they find the ungrateful little---" Stella stopped him. She grabbed the sleeve of his jacket and pulled him toward her. Walt was a big man with broad shoulders and a long torso. He stood well over six feet, and he was surprised by Stella's action.

"They found our daughter in Wyoming," She began. "you did this. Even when she was a little girl you never showed her any love, and as she grew older you treated her like a slave , and I let you. She's the only good thing that's come of this marriage and you drove her off, and I let you. She ran away, Walt. She ran away from us."

Walt stared at Stella like he was seeing her for the first time. She'd always been so docile, and he'd never seen her angry like this. Stella wasn't finished.

"We could lose her, Walt!" Stella said. The state could take her from us, and if she goes I go."

Terresa was a large woman with a large bosom, large hips and a moon face. She wore her hair cut like men generally wore theirs, short on the sides, parted on the left and combed over to the right. Ken on the other hand was tall and slender, balding in the front of his head and had a large black mustache reminiscent of Groucho Marx. When he came home from work he found his wife at the kitchen table, her head buried in her large arms, weeping. He laid his hand on her shoulder, and she stood and engulfed him in her arms.

"They found CeCe," she said as she sobbed. To her surprise ken seemed to be concerned.

" Is she alright," Ken asked. "What about Daniel?" He guided Terresa to a chair at the kitchen table and sat next to her. Terresa shook her head.

"They don't know where he is," she said in a high squeaky voice. "A policeman came by and said that CeCe was in the hands of Child Protective Services somewhere in Wyoming."

"Dear God," Ken said. "I'm sorry, love. I know I was mad about them leaving but I've been worried sick. Do we have to go get her?"

"No," Teresa said, wiping her eyes with the sleeve of her blouse. "The policeman said that we would be hearing from CPS here in Sweetwater and they would be handling things. You think I was too hard on Daniel?"

"You didn't mean him any harm, love," Ken said as he stroked Teresa's arm. "Let's just pray to the Almighty that they find him too."

The call they were waiting for came the very next day. The Texas department of family Services advised them that the girls were in route back to Texas and an appointment was made for Teresa and Walt to meet with an agent.

Paty Thorton was right on time, and with her was her daughter, Sharon Thorton. They almost looked like twins, George thought as they sat side by side in the waiting room. Both Paty and Sharon were red heads. Their facial features were very much the same except that Paty had crow's feet at her eyes. They both wore jackets.

Paty was wearing a stylish black imitation leather with a small roll of fur around the collar that ended at the top loop that held the jacket closed. Loops were around small hooks all the way down to the bottom of the jacket. Her shoes were a high-topped patent leather with round toe. Sharon was wearing a grey hoody and knee-high brown boots that zippered up the inside. After Paty introduced Sharon George spoke to them.

"I thank you ladies for being so prompt," he began. "Ms. Sharon , I'd like to visit with you first and get some basic information." He escorted Sharon into an adjoining office and closed the door. "Please, have a seat," he said as he motioned to a chair in front of his desk. Once seated he obtained some basic information from her. He asked her age to which she said she was thirty-four, she said her height was five six and she weighed somewhere around one hundred or so. He obtained her address and entered her phone number which he already had in his note book.

"Mrs. Thorton, are you employed?" He asked.

"I am," she replied. "I am a manager at a branch of the First State Bank in Frankfurt, Kentucky. I took a few days off to be here with my mother."

" I take it that Mr. Paul Thorton was your father?" George stated his question.

"Yes, of course," Sharon responded.

" How did you find out about the accident that happened on September seventh?" George asked.

" I was at home," Sharon started. "It was about eight-forty-five at night, and I got a call from my mother."

"And what did she say when she called," George continued to probe.

"She said that there had been an accident and that "Pops," that's what I called him, appeared to be seriously injured."

" Did she say how he had been injured?" Was George's next question.

"No," Sharon said. "She just said she found him, and he wasn't moving. She was very upset and wasn't being very coherent. I asked if she had called an ambulance and she said no, she didn't know what to do. So I told her to hang up and I'd call. In my job I have access to phone books from every state, so I looked in the Wyoming phone book under Sweetwater County, and immediately saw the number for the Sheriff's Office and called it."

"I suppose you've had a conversation with your mother about the situation since you've been here, has she told you anything I should know about the accident?" George was fishing.

"I'd just as soon not discuss my private conversations with my mother." Sharon said.

George knew that he'd probably gotten as much information from Sharon that he was gonna get. That last question was a game stopper. He did not want to alienate her; he might need her later.

" One other thing Miss Thorton and I'll let you go," George said. "I checked with his office manager and apparently Mr. Thorton had not kept his regular office hours. Do you know why that was?"

"Oh yes," Sharon began. "Every month he goes to visit his mother in Nebraska. He had gone there and got weathered in. He had just gotten home shortly before the accident happened."

"Do you by chance have his mother's phone number?" George asked.

"Do you have to disturb her at this terrible time.?" Sharon asked.

" If I don't talk to everybody associated with this case," George began. "I won't have done a decent investigation, and there will always be a question. I intend to close this case with nothing lingering."

"Yes," Sharon said. "I have it here in my address book." Sharon took a little green hard cover book from her purse and gave George the number to Mrs. Preston.

"Very good Miss. Thorton," George said rising from his chair. "You have been very helpful in helping me tie things together about which I was wondering. How long are you going to be in town in case I need to speak with you again?"

"I'll be here until we're able to make all the necessary arrangement for my father," Sharon revealed. "They haven't released his body yet so I can't give you an exact range of time."

"I understand," George said as he escorted Sharon back into the waiting room.

Paty Thorton looked tired, and her face lacked any color as she sat herself across the desk from George, and he started out apologizing for having to question her at this time. Then he asked his first question.

"Mrs. Thorton I understand that Mr. Thorton had been away in Nebraska prior to his death. Do you know what he was doing up there?

"Yes," Paty said. "He was visiting his mother, Mrs. Molly Preston. He goes up there almost every month."

"What time did he get home that night, do you remember?" George asked.

"He got in about seven- thirty or seven -forty-five," Paty answered.

"To cover all the basis in my investigation, I'll need to speak with Mrs. Preston," George advised. " Do you by chance have her phone number?"

"Yes of course," Paty said as she took a pen from a cup on the desk and wrote the number on a sticky note pad that was there. George took notice of her fingernails as she wrote the number.. They were not very long but they were longer than he would expect on the hands of a person that did massaging. "I don't understand why there is so much to do about the accident," Paty said showing some frustration. "You people are keeping us from making final arrangements for Paul. How much longer is this taking you think?"

"I promise you," George began. "I'll wrap this investigation up just as soon as I can, just as soon as I have no further questions about what led up to Mr. Thorton's death. For example, there were marks on Mr. Thorntons face that we don't believe were caused by the fall. They were scratches instead of bruises. Any idea about that?"

" I have no idea," Paty said.

"Mr. Thorton got home between seven-thirty pm and seven-forty-five," George noted. "You called your daughter around eight-forty-five. What took place in that hour?"

"This sounds like an interrogation, do I need an attorney," Paty asked.

" Only if Mr. Thornton's death was not really an accident, Mam," George said.

"You think it was other than an accident don't you?" Paty replied. "I think I should not answer any more questions without legal advice. I don't mean to be difficult, but I don't like the way this interview is going. I'll have my attorney contact you." She got up, excused herself and left the room.

CHAPTER 4

Beth and CeCe were only gone a short while when Daniel began to doubt his decision to stay on board the train. The temperature was really not too bad but the air as a result of the trains movement was cold as it flowed through the carrier. He was also hungry and dirty, and he missed the girls already. All of a sudden he was afraid.

As he peered out at the landscape, barren and desolate the train jerked violently and he realized that it was slowing down again. He strained to look in the direction the train was traveling, and he saw a sign that read **THAYER JCT.** After the sign, Daniel could see old mobile homes scattered about the area. There was another jerk, and the train began to move slower. Then there was the trains horn that sounded. It seemed to be so far away. **WAAAAAH-WAAAAH,** IT SOUNDED. **WAAAAUUUAAAAH.** The train was now traveling almost at a crawl . Daniel moved between the carrier he was on and the adjoining one and jumped. He landed on his feet, but the trains momentum caused him to lose his balance and he rolled head over heels in the dirt and bushes.

The train had slowed because of an intersection at this sparsely populated area. Clothing torn and tattered, his hands and face scratched, his hair full of dirt and sticks Daniel made his way to the road that crossed the tracks. A short distance from the intersection he saw a stuccoed building with some red and blue lights in its windows. There was a sign over the door that read, **DUSTY TRAIL CAFÉ.**

Thayer Junction located about twenty-five miles east of the town of Rock Springs, between the Union Pacific rail road tracks and Highway I-80 was the remnants of the days of the oil and gas boom that ended a couple of years past. The streets were unimproved, and the majority of structures were mobile homes. The only permanent type structures were located along its main street, the Dusty Trail Café, a Mercantile that had two gas pumps outside, what was a laundromat and now just a deteriorating wooden building. Like the old laundromat there were several other buildings in disrepair. Daniel moved toward the building with the sign over the door.

There was an old beat -up pickup parked out front and Daniel passed it and entered the Café. There were four small tables with chairs and a bar that ran almost the entire length of the structure. At one end there was a gate that gave access to the building's rear section where there was a kitchen and gave access to the front for workers. Bottles of assorted alcoholic beverages lined the walls behind the bar. A pay telephone hung on the wall at the other end of the bar. A white board on the bar showed what was on the menu.

There was one man sitting at one of the tables and Daniel's eyes locked on a hamburger he was eating. Behind the bar was a very large person wearing overalls. At first Daniel couldn't tell if it was a man or a woman, but as he approached the bar he noticed that there were boobs in the overalls . Her hair was grey on the sides and jet black on top, combed straight back.

"What the hell happened to you boy," the lady asked

" Ma'am, could I have something to eat," Daniel responded as he stood with his hands jammed in the pockets of his jeans.

"How old you be boy?" The lady asked. "You got any money? Where you from boy?" The woman continued to prob. "Ya look like you been in a cat fight, and ya lost."

"I'm sixteen and I jumped off the train," Daniel replied. "I don't have money, but I haven't eaten anything for a long time."

"You a runaway boy?" She asked

"Yes ma'am," Daniel responded.

"Sit down", she said. "I'll make you a couple peanut butter n jelly sandwiches, and stop calling me ma'am, my name is Toby, short for Tobriena. Toby lifted herself off the stool she was sitting on and disappeared into the kitchen. The man sitting at the table had listened intently at the conversation between Daniel and Toby. As Daniel went to one of the other tables the man motioned him to sit with him.

The man wore a baseball type cap that had "Blackbutt Mine" embroidered on the front and he was dressed in a one-piece cover all. He wore his hair in a pony tail that stuck out the back of his cap. When Daniel sat down he spoke with a mouth full of burger.

"Where you from?" he asked.

"Sweetwater, Texas," Daniel said.

"Dam, that's a long way from here aint it?" Was the response. "How long you been on that train?"

" Don't really know," Daniel said. "Three maybe, five days." Daniel began to fidget in his chair.

"By the way, my name is Bart," the man said. "When I was a kid, I ran away once. If there had been a train I might have hopped one, but we lived on a farm, and it was a long way from railroad tracks or a major road. It was lots of woods and stuff. There was a town, maybe five miles from where we lived, and I ran away to town."

"Yeah, what happened?" Daniel was curious.

"I had a dollar fifty cents in my pocket so when I got to town I went to the corner store to buy an ice cream bar. Mr. Parker, the owner, knew I had no business there by myself, so he called my Pa and told him where I was.

"How old were you then?" Daniel asked.

"I think I was about ten or eleven," Bart said. Toby came with the sandwiches and a tall glass of milk. Daniel began to devore them.

Bart was toying with an idea. He began to think that this kid could be an opportunity.

"Say Toby," he said. "After this kid finishes his eats, I'll take him over to my place and get him cleaned up, then we can figure out what to do with him."

"Good idea," Toby said. "He looks pretty ragged."

Bart lived in what had been a single wide mobile home. There had been several additions to it over the years and now it looked like it was at least a three-bedroom home. As Bart pulled up in front of the house, in that old pickup that was in front of the café, Daniel noticed a tall tower behind the house. On top of the tower was a large black thing that fascinated him.

"What's that thing," Daniel asked, pointing to the tower.

"That thing," Bart asked. "you mean that big black thing? That's a rubber bladder. That's what holds the water that I use for my kitchen and the bath room. The sun, when it shines, makes that bladder warm and so the water that comes out it is warm. See those hoses coming out of it. One I use to fill it up and the other lets the water out and into the house."

"Never seen nothing like that before," Daniel said.

"In this country you see lots of strange things that people do to get along," Bart replied.

After he helped Daniel get situated and showed him how to work the shower, Bart took his cloths and put them in the washer. As he watched the cloths through the washing machines window, Bart was cooking up a plan. *This kid could be worth something,* he thought.

After the two ladies, Paty and Sharon Thorton had left, George sat at his desk going over his notes that he took during his conversation with them. He remembered the look in Paty Thorton's eyes when he had said that "she only needed an attorney if the fall was other than an accident." He remembered there was a quick widening of the eyes as if he'd hit a nerve. He dialed the number Sharon had given him.

"Hello," came an answer. "this is Molly."

"Mrs. Preston," George inquired.

"Yes." Was the response.

"This is detective George Stenson with the Sweetwater County Sheriff's office. I'm sorry to bother you at this time but I've been assigned to investigate the accident your son had, and I must ask some questions."

"I understand," she said. "Did you say your name was George?"

"Yes Mam, feel free to call me George," he said.

"All right George, you can call me Molly, what can I do for you?"

"I understand your son visited with you on a monthly basis, is that correct?" was the first question.

"Yes, Paul came here on a weekend each month. He would insure that my medications were set up properly in the dispenser so I wouldn't miss taking them. I don't remember things right anymore. The dispenser has an alarm on it that reminds me when I should take pills. Paul would take care of the lawn---there was a long pause. "And if there was maintenance to be done on the house, he would do that or he would call some of his friends that did that kind of work and have them do it." Again there was a pause and George could hear the sound of sniffling. He waited patiently, then Molly continued. "Sometimes he would take me out to dinner with some of his friends and we'd have such a good time."

"Did Paul take you out to dinner when he was there this month Ma'am?" George inquired.

"Oh yes," Molly answered. We went to dinner with a friend of his, Roberta Farly, they had gone to dental school together.

"I understand that Paul stayed on longer this month because of the weather, is that so?" George asked.

"No, that's not right," Mrs. Preston said firmly. "We had terrible weather Saturday and Sunday morning, but it cleared up Sunday evening and Paul left Monday about ten in the morning. "

"Does he routinely leave about that time on Monday," George asked.

"Yes," Molly replied. "He usually leaves at that time so that he misses the heavy truck traffic, and he would get home about seven in the evening."

"I must have misunderstood," George said. "Please accept my condolences and thanks for talking with me."

"I hope I helped clear things up George and thank you." Molly Preston hung up.

George pulled out his note book and reviewed what he knew about this case. Paul Thorton falls down the stairs in his home, breaking his neck and dying, shortly after returning from a trip to Nebraska where he visited his mother. His return had been delayed by weather supposedly, according to a call he made to his office manager and his wife. According to Mrs. Preston, that was not the case. He left at the normal time like he always did. Question, George thought. Where was he from ten o'clock on Monday until approximately seven o'clock pm on Wednesday? What about Roberta Farly? Does she fit into this picture?"

CHAPTER 5

It was early on Sunday morning and Craig and Martha, still in their night cloths were sitting on the floor at the coffee table in the living room sorting photographs that Craig planned to have made into post cards. Most of them were of scenes that he had captured during the winter months; rock formations with icicles jetting from over- hangs; snow covered mountain foothills; antelope in lines that stretched for miles along the road way fences searching for food. The snow in many places during the winter months had been so deep that wildlife had difficulty finding enough to eat. There were pictures of children playing in the snow; people ice fishing on Flaming gorge reservoir; deer standing among the scrub brush as snow falls, and gorgeous sunsets and sun rises reflecting off snowy vistas.

Katie entered from the kitchen with cups of hot chocolate. She was moving very slowly and deliberately. The cups were on saucers, and she had one stacked upon the other in one hand and a single cup and saucer in the other. Martha got to her feet and took the stacked cups.

"Let me help before this juggling act turns into a disaster," she said.

"Hey, I thought I was doing pretty good," Katie said as she sat her cup on the table and joined them on the floor.

"What have you heard about the girls," Craig asked. Katie had kept in touch with Carolyn, at the Department of Child Protective Services .

"You never get much information out of those people because they're not allowed to divulge much," Katie began. However, I have found out that the girls have been removed from the detention rooms at the hospital and are now under the jurisdiction of the Texas CPS. I don't know where they are. I'm assuming that they are in route to Texas or are already there."

"I think a lot about those kids," Craig said. "When any child is placed in the states systems, I'm not sure we do them any favors. They get bounced around while the agencies take their ever-loving time investigating the conditions that brought them there, and many of them end up in group homes where they learn how to manipulate the system."

"You know Dad," Katie interjected. "I've got a good feeling about these girls. I think because of our involvement so early in the process things will move at an accelerated pace. The group home scenario won't come in to play I think, or if it does it will only be for a very short period of time."

"What we don't know is the other side of the story, about the parents and the home situation," Craig said. "We don't have any idea how long that Texas agency is gonna take with their investigation."

"I have concerns about them too," Martha joined in. "But I think we did the right thing in getting CPS involved. I really feel sorry for little CeCe. She is so worried about her brother, and she feels remorse about leaving him. Any word from Steve? Has he heard anything from the railroad people?"

"Haven't talked to Steve for a while. Maybe tomorrow I'll check with him."

Just as he had said, on Monday morning Craig drove over to the Detention Center and sat down in Steve's office where they both sat sipping coffee from mugs with the sheriffs star embossed on them. Steve was really proud of them and had given one to each employee that worked in the jail and administrative sections. He also had a box full that he intended to give to officials and friends of the department when they visited.

" You guys busy around here?" Craig asked.

"Not really," Steve responded. "Just routine stuff, oh-and we do have an investigation going in the Paul Thorton case."

"Thought that was an accident," Craig commented.

"Geroge aint so sure," Steve said. "He's like a bloodhound. He keeps his nose to the ground and follows the scent until it runs out. He feels that things aren't adding up as you would expect them to. We'll see."

" Have you heard anything from the railroad authorities about the boy that was with the runaway girls?" Craig asked.

"Yeah, a couple days ago. They came up with nothing," Steve said. "Funny you should ask though. I got a call last evening from the Texas Family Protection Agency." Steve paused and took a note book from his pocket. "Someone knows where that kid is."

"How you figure," Craig wanted to know.

"Someone called that boy's parents," Steve began. "They weren't home at the time, but the caller left a message. They were going to send me a fax with some information regarding that. Hold on a minute, let me check." Steve picked up the phone on his desk and pushed the button that connected him to his administrative assistant.

"Yes, sir?" Heather answered.

"Good Morning. Heather," Steve said. "Did we by chance get a fax from the Texas Family Protective Services?"

"Yes, sir," was the answer. "It was in the printer when I came in. Are you ready for me to bring it in?"

"Yes, please," Steve requested. Almost immediately the office door opened, and Heather entered with several pieces of paper in her hands. She took the sheet on top of the stack and gave it to Steve. The others she put in the in box on his desk, then quietly left the room. Steve sat silently reading the fax.

"Well," Craig Said. "Can you share it with me?"

"Yeah, Boss, I'm sorry," Steve apologized. "There was a message left on Mr. and Mrs. Furguson's phone, from a male caller that said. *Your son Daniel is safe. I'm sure you'd like to have him back. What's it worth to you?"*

"That's it?" Craig asked.

"That's it," Steve said. "They sent the information to us because the girls were found here so they suspect that the call was placed from this area."

"That makes sense." Craig said. "I also believe the guy plans to call back."

George wanted to know if Roberta Farley was some way connected. The question that kept nagging at him was, *was Paul Thorton cheating? Did Paty Thorton suspect that he was cheating? Was there an argument that turned into a fight? He* dialed 411 and a female voice responded.

"Information; State, city and the last name of the party you are trying to reach please."

" Nebraska, Bellevue, Last name Farley," George rattled off.

"One moment please", the operator said. After a short pause she continued. "I have three Farly's in Bellevue, A Farley Dental Clinic, Patricia Farley and a Roberta Farley, which number would you like?"

"I'd like the number of the clinic and Roberta Farly, please," George wrote down the numbers and thanked the operator. He noted the time on the clock on his office wall that it was four-thirty in the evening, so he thought he'd give Roberta a call. When he dialed her number he was surprised when she picked right up.

"Hello," she said.

" Am I speaking to Roberta Farly," George inquired.

"Yes, this is freaky," Roberta said. "I was reaching for the phone to make a call when it started ringing. What can I do for you?"

"My name George Stenson," George identified himself. " I'm a detective with the Sweetwater County Sheriff's Office in Green River, Wyoming."

"My!" Roberta exclaimed. "Am I being investigated?"

"No Ma'am," George said. "But I do have a few questions that I hope you have the answers too."

"Well, let's give it a try. She said.

"Are you acquainted with, or do you know Mrs. Molly Preston?" George asked. The question was designed to put her at ease.

"Yes, she's the mother of a very good friend of mine," Roberta related.

"Have you spoken with Mrs. Preston recently," George already knew that she had.

"Why yes, I had dinner with her and her son Paul a couple of nights ago," Roberta said. "What's wrong? Is Mrs. Preston alright?"

"She's fine, Ma'am, I asked you those questions just to verify some information I'd already been told."

"Can you tell me what this is all about?" Roberta Farly asked.

"Yes Ma'am," George replied. "There's been an accident and I'm investigating."

"What's happened? What kind of accident? Who's been hurt?" Roberta sounded irritated.

"Mr. Paul Thorton has been involved in an accident," George related. "Did you see Mr. Thorton after having dinner with him and his mother?"

"I did," she advised. "He spent Tuesday and Wednesday morning working at the Clinic. We have been working on a paper that we are planning to present at the National Association of Dentistry Convention in Washington DC next month. We've been doing a lot over the phone but since he was here we decided that it would be best if we could work together and save a lot of back and forth. The deadline for submission of presentations is two days from now. We finalized it on Wednesday morning, and I sent it by Fedx today. Is Paul alright?"

"Mr. Thorton is deceased, Ms. Farley," there was a sucking sound and a muffled scream at the other end of the line. Then there was a long silence. "Are you all right Ms. Farly?"

"No, I'm not alright," Roberta said. "What happened to Paul?"

"He fell down a flight of stairs Wednesday evening," George said.

" I just talked to him that morning and thanked him for all the work he'd done. We spent a lot of time working on that project. He was so proud of what we'd done. I'll miss him," Roberta said with sadness in her voice.

"Please forgive me Ma'am, but I have to ask a personal question. George paused, and there was nothing said by either party. Then George spoke. "Was there anything other than a working relationship between you and Mr. Thorton?

"No," Roberta said. "There could have been long ago. We were class mates in Dentistry School. We always did work well together, but no, there was no romantic relationship between us. Poor Paty, I'll have to give her a call."

"Thank you for your time Ma'am, and please accept my condolences." George hung up the phone and felt sorry for that lady.

He felt that she had really lost a dear friend. The phone rang and startled him.

"Detective Stenson, can I help you?"

" Yeah George, you remember me. I'm Tony Ward, with Ward, Noble and Dolan law firm. How've you been?"

"Been well Mr. Ward. Haven't seen you since I beat the pants off you in that fraud case last year," George responded.

"you know how it is George," Tony said. "You win some and loose some. Say, I understand you're investigating the Thorton matter. The Thortons have been clients of ours for years and Mrs. Thornton came to me for legal advice after her interview with you."

"She told me that she was going to talk to an attorney," George said.

"Well, I'd like to bring Mrs. Thorton by, I believe she might be able to answer a few of the questions that you may not have answers to yet," Tony said.

"I'll be available first thing in the morning," George advised.

" Good, we'll be there, have a nice day, George," Tony hung up.

Everyone settled in at the morning briefing and were in the briefing room before Steve got there. Tera, Kevin and George were still sipping there coffee out of the new mugs when Steve walked in, coffee mug in hand.

"Good morning to you." Steve said in greeting to them all. "Let's get right to it this morning I think I'm going to have a busy day, Tera, what cha got."

"You'll be glad to know that the girls, CeCe, and Beth that were being housed in the detention facility at the hospital are back in Texas. They were picked up by the Texas Family Protection Agency. For the first time since I've been here there is no one being held in detention,"

Tera related. "Several domestics going to court this morning and two guys picked up on warrants, one out of New Mexico and one out of South Dakota making their first court appearances. That's it for me."

"Kevin? Anything in your area?" Steve asked.

"Nothing pertaining to operations. Things are going pretty smoothly, but I do have an announcement to make," Kevin said, grinning from ear to ear. "Maggie and I are engaged." Everyone expressed their approval and bestowed congratulations. It took a few moments for things to return to normalcy. Even Steve joined the rest. He took a few minutes to explain to Tera and George that Maggie used to be the secretary to the Rock Springs Police Chief, and that Kevin had be courting her for some time.

"Glory be," he said. "I thought it would never happen. OK, Let's get back at it. George you're up."

"I think I'll wrap up the Thorton thing today. I'll be meeting with Mrs. Thorton and her attorney this morning."

"You still feel there's more to this than meets the eye," Steve asked.

"I've been in this business a long time,' George began. "My gut tells me that this wasn't just an accident. I'm sure I'll know what happened after I talk with Mrs. Thorton today."

"Very good," Steve expressing an air of approval for George's work. "Now I've got some news for you. Someone knows where that boy is that was with the two runaway girls that just went back to Texas. The parents received a phone message that indicated that someone was attempting to extort them. The Texas Ranger that's stationed in Sweetwater is working with the telephone company, trying to track down where the call was made from. That's what I'll be working on today. George, good luck, Kevin I'm really happy for ya, as sheriff Spence would say, Lets go to work."

It was a little after ten am when Paty Thorton and Tony, her attorney, showed up in the waiting room outside George's office. He greeted them warmly and escorted the two of them into his office.

" Sorry for tying up your morning, George," Tony said, apologizing. "I'm sure you expected us earlier."

"I have nothing planned that would interfere with an opportunity to visit with you and your client , Mr. Ward, George said."

"Mrs. Thorton wishes to fill you in with some information that she neglected or was reluctant to convey to you at her last visit," Tony begam. "I want you to understand, that the information my client provides you is not an admission of any wrong doing on her part nor does she entertain that she in anyway contributed to the accident that resulted in her husband's death."

"Would you object to me recording what Mrs. Thorton has to say?" George asked. "And you, Mr. Ward, can make that same statement on the recording before Mrs. Thorton begins to speak. Fair enough?"

"Fair enough," Tony said. George removed a recording machine from his desk draw and positioned the microphone so that is would best pick up Tony' and Paty's voice. Once he had everything set he turned on the machine and started the conversation. He identified himself, stated the date, and the investigation that the recording pertained to. He identified all those present and asked Tony to make his statement. He did. Then he asked Mrs. Thorton opening questions.

"Would you please state your full name Mrs. Thorton?"

"Paty Marie Thorton," she said.

"And you reside at 2704 Canyon, place in Green river, Wy. is that correct?"

"That's correct," Paty agreed.

"Were you at that residence on the night in question when Mr. Thorton had an accident," George asked.

"I was and I'll never forget it," Paty said.

"Just answer his question," Tony admonished.

"Paul was in Nebraska and had informed me that he would be delayed returning because of the weather," Paty began. " When I arrived home from my massage establishment on Tuesday evening I checked the house phone to see if Paul had left any messages. I expected that he would call and let me know if he was able to start for home. There was no message. I then thought that maybe, just maybe he might have left a message on the office phone upstairs. There was no message there either. I accidentally struck the caller ID button, and it startled me when it flashed on. It displayed a call from his office manager, one from Beta Insurance, one from Roberta, one from Bob Mason his financial adviser and another from Roberta. I scrolled through the caller ID and noticed several more calls from Roberta. Who is Roberta? I thought. It troubled me all through the night and all-day Wednesday." She paused to catch her breath, then continued.

"By the time Paul came in on Wednesday evening I had worked myself to a frenzy. He had no sooner put his luggage down when I confronted him."

"Why didn't you call me yesterday and let me know how things were?" I asked.

"I didn't think you would worry, since I'd already told you I'd be delayed," Paul said.

"You didn't think," I said. "And by the way, who is Roberta?"

"She's a colleague," Paul answered as he started up the stairs to the office. I followed.

"How come you've never mentioned her before?" I asked. "Where does she live?"

"Didn't think it was important," Paul said as he put his bag in a closet.

"Did you she her while you were up there," I asked.

"As a matter of fact, Mom and I had dinner with her Sunday night," Paul responded as he moved past me toward the stairs. "Since I was there anyway I spent Tuesday working with her on a project."

" And Tuesday night?" I was insistent and grabbed Paul's arm turning him to face me.

"As a matter of fact, we worked late and I caught a nap in one of her dental chairs," Paul replied.

" What's going on with you and that woman Paul, I remember screaming. Why are you lying to me?" At that point I slapped him across the face. I guess it caught Paul off guard, and I watched as things happened in slow motion. Paul began to fall backwards, trying to catch himself by reaching for the lattice work along the stair case as he slid down the stairs and crashed into the wall at the landing. I stood frozen. I screamed.

"Paul! Paul!" I ran down the stairs. "Paul are you alright," I asked. Paul was making strange sounds in his throat, but he didn't answer, nor did he move. I tried to move him, but he was too heavy. Then the noises stopped.

I sat on the landing, just starring at Paul lying there, so still and his eyes were open, starring back at me, accusing me. I sat there a long time before I finally realized that something had to be done. But what? I thought. What was I supposed to do? I decided to call my daughter, she'd know what to do."

Paty slumped down in the chair in which she sat, looked at Tony then at George and softly said. "That's the way it happened. "

"I'll give this tape to our office assistant, and she'll transcribe it for us," George stated. "It'll only take a few minutes, and I'll have you sign the statement that you just gave us. I will then put my report together and drop it off at the District Attorney's office. That office will take it from here. I want to thank you Paty and you Tony for your cooperation in this."

"It's obvious to me that it was just a tragic accident," Tony said. "Hope Paty will now be able to mourn in peace and put this thing behind her."

"I'm sure the DA will keep you informed Mr. Ward," George said as he stood and moved to the door. "Thank you for coming in and I wish you a nice day." Tony shook George's hand as he departed, and Paty just moved swiftly passed him with not as much as a smile.

As he periodically did, Steve was having lunch with Craig and Martha at the Senior Manor of Green River. They were serving lasagna today, a dish that was not Craig's favorite and he had asked Martha never to feed it to him, so he had a cheese burger while Steve and Martha enjoyed their Lasagna.

"How are the girls doing?" Martha was asking.

"You know," Steve began. "I'm so proud of those two. Milly has really overcome that injury to her leg and not holding back at all. She has a limp but it's not extreme. She's all set to start her new job at the National Park. We got her another car, not a new one but a program car, you know, one that had been used as a demonstrator, had a little over four thousand miles on it."

"What did you get her?" Craig inquired.

"A 1987 Jeep Rangler," Steve responded. " She likes it, and it will serve her well in that country."

"Everyone still ok at the shop?" Craig asked.

" Oh yeah, and you'll be glad to know that Kevin and Maggie are engaged," Steve related. Martha clapped her hands together and exclaimed, "OH Good Heavens!"

"I wondered how long it would take for her to get over her bad experience." Craig commented.

"I commend Kevin for being patient and giving her the time she needed," Martha stated. Their conversation was interrupted by Steve's radio sputtering.

"SO1, Dispatch, a voice said. Steve answered. "SO1, go ahead."

"SO1 are you near a land line," the dispatcher asked.

"Can be in a minute," Steve responded.

"SO1 give dispatch a call," was the request.

"10-4 dispatch, give me a minute," Steve said as he got to his feet.

"There's a pay phone in the lobby," Craig advised. "Or I'm sure the manager will let you use their phone if you think you might need some privacy." Steve moved quickly toward the lobby and Martha spoke up.

"Sure is nice that you don't have to get those kind of calls anymore."

"You know," Craig began. "After all this time, I still kinda miss it, but I'm not sure I'd ever want to do it again." Steve was returning to the table and Craig inquired.

"Do you have to leave?"

"No, Kevin just got a call from the Texas Child Protection agency. They traced the call. It was made from a pay phone out in Thayer Junction," Steve said.

"Thayer Junction," Craig recalled. "That little burg always had an aversion for law enforcement. I never could get any cooperation from anyone out there."

"It hasn't changed," Steve offered. "I think they must have some type of alert system that warns everyone when a cruiser or a strange vehicle is in the area. When we try to serve bench warrants that whole area all of a sudden goes dark. Nobody will talk to you and when you knock on doors , there's nobody home."

"As I recall there is only one Pay phone out there and it's in the Café," Craig remembered. "The last I recall that café was closed."

"Yeh, it was closed for a while," Steve said. "There was a mine accident, and a woman lost her husband, She got a pretty good settlement, and she reopened it."

"I've got an idea," Craig announced. "There are several old mine shafts out there that still have the remnants of the old, abandoned derricks and sloughs of the old mines still standing. I've been wanting to go out there and take some pictures of that stuff. This would be a good time to do that, and I Could nose around."

"You just can't keep that nose of yours out of things can you," Martha said sternly. "Steve, tell him to stay out of the way."

"I would Martha, except I think it's a great idea," Steve said. "I doubt that there is anybody out there anymore that would recognize him. I really don't have anybody that I can spare to go snooping around out there. I do think I'd want to deputize you boss, just in case.

"Just in case what?" Martha asked.

"Just in case it becomes necessary for that guy to be detained," Steve explained. "You never know how these things might develop."

"I Should have known better than to expect any help from you," Martha said. "You're both like two peas in a pod. If you do this Craig, you just snoop, nothing else."

" I promise," Craig said. "If I find out anything I'll use that payphone and call Steve. That ok with you, Steve?"

"That'll be perfect, and I'll take it from there," Steve agreed.

The next day the sun was out and the snow on the dirt roads on the plateaus around Green River had turned to slush, Craig took his jeep and drove it several miles along a seldom traveled road used by the Forest service and got it plenty dirty.

Early the following morning he loaded his camera cases in the jeep, checked to make sure his 357 was in the glove compartment, and put a large envelope containing some of his post cards and pictures, that he intended to make cards out of, in the pocket behind the driver's seat. He made sure the badge Steve had given him was in his breast pocket. Muddy water had dried on the jeeps windshield, so he turned on the wipers, and watched as they made an arch on both the drivers and passengers side.

As he approached Thayer Junction, he checked his watch. It was nine thirty and he figured the people that worked at the mines would have already left and there would be few people around. He could see the café and there were only a couple of pickups parked there. He parked the jeep in an open spot and went in.

There were three female patrons at the tables, two together and one sitting alone. Craig decided to take a seat at the bar where he could see the entire interior of the place. Sitting on her stool, at one end of the bar was a person in overhauls. Could have been male or female, but Craig noticed it had boobs.

"Mornin," She said. "What'll ya have?"

"I could use a cup of coffee," Craig replied. She slid off her stool and went into the kitchen. When she returned she had a ten-cup size coffee pot. She reached under the counter and placed a thick mug in front of Craig and filled it with coffee. As she poured she spoke to Craig.

"I'm Toby. Don't remember seeing you around before," she said. "Where you from?"

"Green River," Craig answered.

"What cha doin way out here?" She asked.

"I'm a photographer," Craig replied. "I take pictures and make post cards, Wanna see some?" Craig opened the envelope and spread some of the pictures on the counter. Toby picked through them one at a time.

"Them's pretty pictures," Toby said. "Them's nice cards too. What you taking pictures of out here?"

" You know those old, abandoned oil rigs and mining slews up the road a piece, I'll be taking pictures around them and of them," Craig said. He sipped his coffee and watched Toby's face over the rim of his cup. She was still picking through the pictures. "I've got some more," he said as he dumped the remaining pictures in the envelope on the counter. Toby sat the coffee pot off to the side and continued looking.

"Them old things out there make good pictures?" she asked. "They just rusty metal and rotten wood."

" That's what makes them interesting," Craig said.

"OK," Toby said as she picked up the pot, poured more coffee in Craig's cup and went back into the kitchen. Craig busied himself putting the pictures and cards back into the envelope. Toby returned to her stool.

"It's been years since I was out here," Craig stated. "Many people live here now?"

"Maybe fifty," Toby replied. "They come n' go. Since the mines cut back few people live out here anymore."

"I suppose not many visitors come through here either, huh?" Craig commented. Toby chuckled.

"You the only visitor I've seen in months," she said. "The only person we see that don't live here is the mail man and he only comes if somebody gets a letter or package. Oh, and we did get a runaway come in a couple of days ago. Jumped off the train when it came through."

" A runaway huh?" Craig said as he emptied his cup of coffee and stood up to leave. "Guess I'd better get out there while the sun is still out. "Guess that runaway is still on the run huh?"

"No," Toby said. "I fed him and one of the guys took him in and cleaned him up. I guess he'll keep him until he decides what to do with him."

"Well, I'm off," Craig said as he placed two dollars on the counter and picking up his envelope. "Maybe I'll stop in again on my way out. Keep the coffee hot." Craig walked out and got into the jeep. He could see Toby watching him as he backed the jeep out.

CHAPTER 6

CeCe and Beth were getting a taste of life in a group home, while the Texas Department of Family Protective Services determined their future. Like most homes of this type, the home had a set of house parents who supervised their very being twenty-four hours a day. There are negative effects of group homes. Children face isolation and prison-like conditions; limitations on privacy and bathroom use; poor food quality and feeling lonely, unsafe and unloved.

There were only eight girls in the home and CeCe and Beth were separated most of the time. They only saw one another at meals where they were required to eat quietly and learned from other residents how to communicate without talking. CeCe had indicated to Beth, who sat across the dining room table from her, that she thought the food was yucky by pointing at the plate and then sticking her finger in her open mouth and then acting as if she was throwing up. Beth shook her head in agreement. There was one other time when they could talk to each other and that was the hour that they were allowed outside in the buildings court yard.

There were bunk beds for those living at the home and Beth spent lots of time in her bunk which was the middle one between two others. She had lots of time to think about her life at home. She missed her mom. She loved her dad, but she didn't want to live like before. When she had been interviewed by a counselor she had said that.

Beth took a liking for her bunk mate that was in the bunk above her. The girls name was Marcy, and she too was a runaway. Often during the day Marcy would hang her head over the edge of her bunk and she and Beth would tell each other their life stories. Marcy was seventeen years old, and she had run away because her mom's boyfriend was sexually abusing her. Marcy's story sounded so awful to Beth.

CeCe just wanted to go home. She couldn't help feeling that she had failed Daniel by leaving him alone. That feeling ate at her every minute of the day. She cried a lot, and she was afraid that her mom and dad would blame her for Daniel being lost. Because she was smaller than the other girls in her bunk pod, she was on the top bunk. The girl below her was Marline, and they quietly shared their stories after the nine pm lights out at night.

Walt and Stella appeared before an agent for the Texas Department of Family Protective Services after receiving a notice to show cause and explain why their daughter should not be removed from the current family environment.

"This is a hearing to show cause," the agent began. "Being conducted on December 12, 1987, at fourteen hundred hours, at the offices of the Texas Department of Family Protective Services, Located at 1425 Monument Avenue, Sweetwater, Texas, in the interest of Bethea (Beth) Ferguson. Those present are the parents of Bethea-Walt and Stella Ferguson. Mr. and Mrs. Ferguson this hearing is being held to determine if the home environment that Bethea has been exposed to, and that resulted in her running away is such that this agency should step in and in her behalf and possibly exercise our authority to insure her wellbeing."

Stella sat stiffly; her eyes fixed on the face of this female person who has the authority to take her child from her. Walt too sat erect, listening intently at what this person was saying. He felt small and vulnerable in her presence.

"My name is Dorothy Mosely," she continued. "I'll be conducting this interview, and I want you to understand that this is not an adversarial situation. I'm here to represent Bethea but also to assess the situation as it pertains to her future and your ability to participate in her future or not. Please feel free to express yourself and let me know exactly your feelings and your past affiliation with your daughter. Do both of you understand?" Stella and Walt both indicated that they did.

"I also want to advise you that these proceedings are being recorded," Dorothy advised. "Do either of you have an objection to that?" Walt and Stella both said that they didn't.

"Mr. Ferguson," Dorothy began. "What was your relationship with your daughter like?"

"Poor," Walt said fidgeting in his chair.

"Explain please," Dorothy requested.

"I did not treat her very well," Walt revealed.

"Did you abuse her?" Dorothy asked.

"Yeh, I'd say so," Walt responded.

"Tell me about how you abused her," Dorothy said.

"Since Beth left I've had lots of time to mull over this," Walt said. "I never, since she was a little girl, acted like I cared for her. I know now that I treated her like some kind of servant. I drank a lot. Generally after coming home from work and on weekends. I would make her get me beer and pour it in the glass for me. Sometimes the head would boil over on the table, and I would slap her for doing it. I yelled at her a lot."

"Mrs. Ferguson," Dorothy turned to Stella. "Did you contribute to similar abuse of your daughter?"

"I think I did worst," Stella spoke with emotion in her voice. "I allowed Walt to treat her that way. I stood by while he disrespected

Beth and treated her like some slave, not like a daughter. Beth and I had a great relationship otherwise though."

"What has the relationship between the two of you been like," Dorothy asked. "Mr. Ferguson you go first."

" There were times when I had had lots to drink that I was verbally abusive to Stella. I never laid a hand on her though. Beth running off has really made me wake up to what a jerk I've been and how badly I've treated my family. I've always concentrated on work and drinking, never really caring for my family like I should have."

"There is more too," Stella spoke up. "Walt got involved with a church group that is like a cult. They believe that females are worth less than males and even children, males and females are treated differently. This religious belief played a large part in Walts behavior."

"Why should this agency consider placing Beth back into such a dysfunctional situation," Dorothy asked.

"I've already changed. I'm no longer drinking. I now realize that Beth is probably the best thing that has come out of this marriage. I love my wife. Without her I would've been nothing."

"I know you say you've stopped drinking," Dorothy said. "It has been my experience that heavy drinkers will quit for a while but without help, go right back to their old habits sooner than later. Would you be willing to join an AA type organization?"

"I'll do whatever it takes if I can have a second chance with my family," Walt said with tears welling in his eyes.

"You are currently employed, Mr. Ferguson?" Dorothy asked.

"Yes ma'am." Walt replied. "I make good money."

"Mrs. Ferguson," Dorothy continued. "Your past involvement in Beth's life does not show that there would be much protection for Beth should things not go well with Mr. Ferguson's behavior. Why should this agency take such a chance on Beth's future wellbeing?"

"Walt and I have already had that conversation. He has promised to stop drinking and to divorce himself from that religious group. If he fails to keep his promises, Beth and I will continue our lives without him. I will not subject her to any conditions that will affect her in a negative way."

" At a convenient time for you," Dorothy said. "I would like to make a home visit before rendering my recommendations to my superiors."

"Any time you like," Stella said. "Walt will be working but I'll be there."

The hearing concluded very amiably but Walt and Stella were shaken at the possibility that their proposed efforts to turn things around might not be enough to persuade the agency to let Beth stay with them. For Stella, the thought of losing Beth was debilitating. In Walts case, for the first time that he could remember, he was scared.

This time Ken and Terresa were at home when the call came. It was in the evening and Ken answered the phone. The voice on the other end was that of a male and he spoke quietly and sounded as if he was holding something over his mouth, it was muffled.

"I left you a message," he said.

"You said you knew where my son was," Ken blurted out.

"Yeh," the man said. "I guess you'd like to have him back, right?"

"Of course, where is he?" Ken wanted to know.

"Whoa!" the individual exclaimed. "Not so fast. It'll cost you five thousand dollars to get me to tell you where he is. I'll call you back tomorrow, be ready to do business." There was a dial tone, and he was gone.

"Dear God, help me," Ken said.

"What's going on," Terresa asked.

"The man that knows where Daniel is wants five thousand dollars," Ken informed her.

"We need to call that lady from the agency," Teresa said. "She'll know what to do."

Heather, the receptionist at the Sweetwater Sheriff's Office received a call from Dorothy Mosely shortly after she arrived at the office. Dorothy explained why she was calling, and Heather passed the call to Kevin. The call would make him late for the morning briefing, but he knew it was important that he get all the information.

Steve was listening to Tera, the jail administrator, when Kevin walked in the conference room.

"Well," Steve said sarcastically. "Nice that you could join us."

" Sorry I'm late Sheriff," Kevin apologized. "I was on the phone with the Texas Family Protective Services. There has been a new development in the case of that boy that ran away from down there."

"What's going on now," Steve asked.

"The boy's parents got a call from Thayer Junction," Kevin began. "The caller indicated that it would cost them five thousand dollars before he would tell them where the kid is."

"Now we're dealing with extortion," George advised.

"Because that place is such an anti-law enforcement environment, our old boss is doing some snooping for us out there," Steve explained. " I'll be visiting with him this evening to see what he was able to find out. George, why don't you ride over with me, I think I want you to work with Sheriff Spence on this. Stop by my office after the briefing and I'll bring you up to date on the matter."

As he promised, Craig stopped back by the Café as he was on his way out. There were several pickup trucks parked outside and Craig parked his jeep across the street in front of the old laundromat. He had one of his cameras hanging around his neck when he entered the café. There was music coming out of a couple of speakers at each end of the room. There was no room at the bar, so Craig took a seat at the first table. Toby was just coming out of the kitchen with a couple of plates with hamburgers on them as he sat down, and she spotted him.

"Hey there," she said. "Didn't really expect to see you back here." She placed the burgers down in front of one of the men at the bar, and he heard the guy ask for a to-go- box for one of the burgers.

"I told you I might stop in when I headed out," Craig said. "Is the coffee hot?"

"You betcha," Toby replied. She went behind the bar and the coffee pot was now on a warming plate there. As she poured his coffee she asked, "Did you get some good pictures?"

"You know I was pleasantly surprised," he said. "There are a lot of interesting structures out there. I think I may come back tomorrow. The light petered out on me today."

Toby returned to her stool behind the bar, and she was conversing with the individual who had asked for a go box. He heard her say to him, "What does he do all day" and the fellow answered, "Watch TV and snack on chips, pretzels and stuff that I keep around". He took a bite out of his burger and left his perch at the bar and moved to the payphone at the end.

Craig watched as the man took a slip of paper out of the breast pocket of his coveralls and put a coin in the phone. He waited a second or two then reached in his pocket and pulled out a handful of quarters and began putting coins in the slot on the phone. He began talking but Craig thought it strange that he was holding his hand over his mouth. Craig rested his camera on the table, aimed it at the person on the payphone and took several pictures. The call only lasted a short while, and the man returned to his seat at the bar. He heard Toby pick up her conversation.

"Did you get ahold of somebody about him?"

"I made a couple of calls but so far the line is always busy," the guy said.

"How long are you gonna keep him?" Toby was asking.

"If I don't get anybody tomorrow, I'll take him into Rock Springs and turn him over to the cops," he said.

Craig finished his coffee, placed two dollars on the table, waved at Toby and went to his jeep. He took a small pad out of the console between the seats and noted what he had observed and heard. He was pretty sure he had witnessed something relating to the runaway. As he drove back to Green River he kept playing what he had seen and heard over and over in his head. *This is kinda fun,* he was thinking.

As he pulled out onto interstate eighty, he called Martha on the CB radio.

"Hey Doll, come on," he said. He waited for a few minutes, and she answered.

"Are you on your way home? Come on." Martha sometimes used the lingo.

"Just on the highway heading in. Too late for dinner there- how about Pizza? Come on."

"I'll have some delivered," Martha said. "you won't have to pick it up. Be careful, see ya."

Craig made one stop at the photo shop to drop off the film in his camera. He was sure Steve would want to see what the person looked like that was probably responsible for making calls to Texas. He had finished his pizza and was relating to Martha what had gone on during his trip to Thayer Junction when there was a knock on the door. Craig suspected it to be Steve, and it was, and another person that Craig had not seen before.

"Hi, ya Steve, come on in," Craig said. "Come on in. Who's this you got with you?"

"Detective Stenson," Steve introduced George. "I'm assigning him to the case so I brought him over to meet you and hear whatever you may be able to tell us.

Craig introduced George to Martha and took them to the kitchen so as not to disturb Martha who was watching a wrestling match on TV.

"There was a call to the boy's parents today," Steve began. "The caller is demanding five thousand dollars from them to know where there son is. So now we're talking about extortion. Were you able to get any indication that the kid might be out there and where his where abouts might be, Boss?"

Craig related to Steve and Detective Stenson what he had observed and heard while at the café. He also passed the notes that he had taken to the detective.

"I dropped the film off at the photo shop on the way in," Steve said. "I'll pick up the prints first thing in the morning. Based on what you guys have told me, I'm sure that the fella in the pictures was making that call to Texas. The conversation I heard between him and Toby, the café owner, would make me think that the boy is in no danger. If the guy is asking for money to tell where he is, the suspect certainly isn't going to harm him. I'm planning on going back out there tomorrow. I believe I might be able to find out from Toby where that boy might be. If I can, that should give you enough information to request a search warrant, don't you think?"

" I'd like to get that kid pretty quick," George said. "How will you let me know what you find out?"

"I still remember the phone number to the office," Craig said with a chuckle. "I'll find a pay phone and call you."

"You have any idea how best and when to execute a warrant, Boss?" Steve wondered.

"Everybody out there works in one of the mines," Craig said. "The suspect was in the café about five o'clock in the evening, so he works the morning shift. He wears a baseball cap with Black Butt on it. There's a sign in the café window that says she closes at six, so I'd think any time after six."

"I'll get everything ready on the request for a warrant except the guy's name and the address where you say the boy probably is," George said. "you think this guy will put up a fight? How many officers you think I better bring out there with me."

"If we do this right, we'll have surprise on our side," Craig said. "There is always the probability that he'll rabbit, so I suggest you bring a couple of young guys in case there's a chase, you don't look like you'd do well at that, and I know I wouldn't." They all three had a good laugh.

After the daily briefing George was going through the papers in his inbox. Heather always delivered the mail while everyone was in the briefing. He came across a letter from the office of the County Attorney. It was addressed to the Sweetwater County Sheriff's office, to his attention. The subject read, RE: case # 87907-20079 State of Wyoming vs Paty V. Thorton. The letter summarized all of the particulars of the case, the description of the untimely death of Paul Thorton and then the last paragraph which stated the County Attorney's findings. It read, *"After due review and consideration of the referenced case stated above, it has been determined that the death of Mr. Paul Thorton was an unfortunate accident. After reviewing the facts in the investigation conducted by your department, this office finds no evidence that the person of interest, Paty V. Thorton-who also was the decedents wife, willfully or with intent acted in a manner that directly caused the death of Paul Thorton, her husband. It is the intent of this office not to bring charges against Paty V. Thorton or anyone else connected to this case. "*

George leaned forward in his chair, holding the letter at arms-length, he re-read it. It wasn't the first time that he saw things differently than the County Attorney and he was sure it wouldn't be the last. He did understand their thinking, however. Where he in a position to make the call, he would've brought involuntary manslaughter charges. His thinking was if she hadn't slapped him he wouldn't't've fallen. He filed the letter and spent the rest of the morning preparing his request for a search warrant.

CHAPTER 7

After picking up the prints from the photo shop, Craig walked into the café in Thayer Junction around mid-morning. The place was empty except for Toby who was perched on her favorite stool in her favorite spot, reading a book. She folded the book when Craig took a spot at the counter.

"Well," she said. "You're becoming a regular." She moved to the warmer and returned with the coffee pot and a mug.

"There's a couple more scenes I think will make great post cards that I want to take while the lights good, not very busy today huh?"

"Never this time of day," Toby replied. "It's early in the morning around six o'clock till seven, a few of the wives come in around noon. Some of them sit around and play cards for a couple of hours and then the guys start coming in around three thirty till five thirty, depending of what shift they work, and I close up at six."

"At that rate how do you keep going," Craig asked.

"The gas keeps payin' the bills," She said. "This place keeps me sane. Don't expect to get rich, its therapeutic." Craig sipped his coffee holding the mug with both hands. He decided to keep a conversation going.

"How'd you come to have this place, Toby?" he asked.

"It was five or so years ago, my husband died in an accident down in mine number one over in Reliance. The inspectors said that the accident happened because of poor ventilation so I sued. The Union and Pacific Rail Road settled rather than go to court. I needed to get out of Reliance and one of my husband's friends told me about this place. It was boarded up and filthy. It took me a few months to get it in shape and I have a little apartment in back so I'm good. Everybody out here looks after me and they're now my family. I never had kids."

"The man you were talking with yesterday when I was here," Craig asked. "What's his name?"

"Who, Bart?" She replied. "Bart Manning, he works out at the Black Butt mine. He's one that stops in every evening."

"I took a picture of him yesterday in his coveralls and bandana under his cap. Thought it might look good on a card. I changed my mind and decided to stick with structure and natural stuff.. I want to give it to him, but I don't want to have to stay out here till late. Does he live somewhere close, I'll just put it in his mail box."

"There' a group of mail boxes on the next corner up, his number is thirty-six, Toby said. You can just stick it in there." Craig finished his coffee, put two one-dollar bills on the counter and slid off the stool.

"Well," he said. "Gotta go. You take care and maybe I'll stop by again sometime."

"You do that now," Toby said as she picked up the money and the mug.

Craig drove up to where the mail boxes were and put a copy of the picture in number thirty -six. He had had four copies made so he could spare one. The picture was of Bart making that phone call.

Craig spent a couple hours crawling around the old mine slews and remnants of a train spur that was overgrown with tumble weed, but Craig lined it up with some of the deteriorating structures and the rolling hills and the scene told an interesting story.

He drove around checking numbers on the mobile homes and the few houses in the area. He found the double-wide with number thirty-six on it. He took several pictures of it. The closest place with a pay phone other than the café was Point of Rocks, so he drove there and called George at the SO.

It was seven o'clock at night when three unmarked cars from the SO entered the small community of Thayer Junction. Darkness had set in and with lights out the entourage moved slowly, following the directions that Craig had provided, until they approached number thirty-six. George positioned one car on each end of the double-wide and he parked his car directly in front. Using his units radio he gave the command, and they flooded the double wide with headlights and the vehicle spot lights. He spoke on his loud speaker.

"Bart Manning, this is the Sweetwater County Sheriff's Office. Open the door and everyone inside come out with your hands up!" George waited, keeping an eye on the windows and the front door. He repeated his demand. **" Bart Manning, open the front door slowly and everybody inside come out with your hands up!"**

The door partially opened. George could only see the head of a male person through the opening.

"What do you want," the person inquired.

" Are you Bart Manning?" George asked over the loud speaker. **" I have a search warrant, and I need you to come out voluntarily or we're prepared to force our way in. Come out with your hands up!"**

"Yes, I'm Bart Manning, What do you want," Bart asked as he opened the door and shielded his eyes from the lights. He stepped out on the small porch in front of the house and George, the deputies he had brought with him, exited their cars. Two of them took Bart by his arms and led him away from the mobile home and handcuffed him . Another of the deputies stuck a copy of the warrant in Bart's hip pocket and then entered the structure. In just a few moments the deputy came out with the boy.

"Are you Daniel Parsons," George asked.

"Yes," Daniel answered, now visibly shaking in fear.

"It's ok, Daniel," George assured him. "We're going to take care of you."

"I don't want to go home, " Daniel said and his face becoming distorted as he began to cry.

"It'll be all right son," George said as he helped Daniel down the stairs and led him to his car. He put Daniel in the back of his car where there were no handles that he could use to open the door. He then turned to Bart.

'Mr. Manning, You're under arrest for trying to extort Daniel's family. Please understand that you have the right to remain silent; anything you say can and will be used against you in a court of law; you have the right to an attorney during any questioning; if you can't afford an attorney one can be appointed for you. Do you understand your rights?

"Yeh," Bart responded. "What have I done wrong? I took care of that boy. I didn't kidnap him or anything."

"Mr. Manning," George interrupted. "I'm advising you to remain silent. But if you wish to speak about this I'll listen."

The deputies holding onto Bart moved him to one of their cars. George went into the house, Checked the back door to make sure it was locked, turned off all the lights and set the lock on the front door so it would lock behind him. He got into his vehicle and led the way out of the community onto the highway and to Green River detention center. On the way Daniel continued to sniffle, and George tried to keep him conversing.

"Why'd you run away from home Daniel?" he asked.

"My mother always beat on me," Daniel responded.

"Did you do things that made her mad at you?" George asked.

"No, never," Daniel assured. "She said I never did anything right, and she beat on me."

"That must have been some trip on that train. Where were you trying to go?" George continued to prob.

"Didn't know," the boy replied. "Didn't care, just wanted to get away. My sister was with me, but she got off the train with her friend. She always helped me, but her friend got mad at me because I wouldn't get off the train. They were cold and hungry, and they didn't want to go as bad as I did, I guess."

"What made you get off here?" George asked.

I was dirty, cold and hungry, and I got scared cause I was alone. Never been alone before. CeCe, my sister, was always there." Daniel began to cry again. "I miss her. I don't know where she is. You know where my sister and her friend Beth is?"

"Yep," George responded. "They're okay. Both of them are back in Sweetwater I think."

"I don't want to go back to Sweetwater. I want to see CeCe, but I don't want to go near my house," Daniel said emphatically. "What will you do with me?"

"You hungry?" George asked, avoiding the question.

"No, Bart made some tuna sandwiches before you came," was the reply.

"Are those the only clothes you have?" George was looking at Daniel through the rearview mirror."

"Yeh, I didn't bring any other stuff with me," Daniel said.

" Looks like you didn't plan this very well Daniel," George admonished softly.

"Guess not, just wanted to get away," Daniel said.

"Why did your sister go with you?" George asked. "Was she beat on too?"

"No, CeCe never got beat on. When I said I was gonna run away she said she was going with me. CeCe is the only one what cared about me. I wish she was here now," Daniel said.

While the other cars drove into Green River where they would book Bart into the County Jail, George broke off in Rock Springs and drove directly to the hospital where he processed Daniel into the detention section. George stayed with Daniel until he was all settled in the room that he would be held in until Child Protective Services could get involved.

The morning briefing went off right on schedule and Steve applauded sarcastically when he came into the conference room, and everyone was seated around the big table.

"We'll have to chalk this one up for the ages," he said with a grin. "Tera, let's let you get started and tell us what's going on in the jail today."

"Sheriff," Tera began. "We're full up. There was a full moon last night and I guess all the crazies came out of hiding. We have everything from attempted murder to sexual assaults to take to court today. George and his crew brought in a fellow last night that we helped find a lawyer. He can afford one, but he just didn't know any because he's never needed one. We gave him a list and there's one with him as we speak so I expect he might bond out after he's arraigned today."

"What's the ratio, male to female," Steve asked.

"About thirty- seventy," tera responded. "Thirty being the female side. We've got somebody in every cell, including the drunk tank."

"You need any additional help?" Steve asked.

"I've already called in a couple part timers to bolster the staff," Tera replied.

"Good move," Steve commented. "Kevin, I guess you and your patrol deputies are somewhat responsible for our occupancy status."

"It was a strange night for sure," Kevin began. "Started out early with a group of kids in the Walmart parking lot cutting donuts. Apparently three vehicles, loaded with kids, were whippin' around the lot at the same time when two of them collided. One of the cars, a Dodge Charger, rolled over pinning three occupants under it. They had life-threatening injuries but were alive when they got to the hospital. The other vehicle, a Nesan pickup, didn't roll, but it sustained serious damage. There were kids riding in back and they were all thrown out. All of them had scrapes and bruises, nothing serious. There was a young man leaning out of the passenger door window and was caught between the two cars when they came together. He didn't make it. Both drivers were unhurt and were arrested." Kevin flipped some pages in a note book he carried and then continued.

"I'm sure you remember Shara Smith," Kevin said through a sheepish grin. "She's that little lady that looks like Mrs. Santa Clause that gets drunk and beats up on her husband. Well, he called again asking for help. She generally used a frying pan or some other kitchen pot, but this time he said she was using a crow bar to chase and hit him with. Deputy Morris was sent on the call and when he got there Mr. Smith had locked himself in the bath room and Shara was trying to pry the door open with the crow bar, but she was so drunk she was having trouble getting it in the space between the door and the door frame. The Smiths live in a mobile home and Deputy Morris could see what was happening through the front window. The front door was standing open, so he entered and took the bar away from Shara, let Mr. Smith out of the bath room and decided to bring Shara down here. As usual, we expect Mr. Smith to come down and bail her out after she sobers up." There was laughter around the table because all had at one time, or another dealt with Shara Smith. Kevin wasn't through.

"The funny part about the Shara Smith incident was the trip down here. Deputy Morris got her in the back of his unit without any problem, but she smelled so bad he put the rear windows down half way. She was cuffed so he wasn't concerned about her trying to get out. This was his first time dealing with Shara, so he didn't know that she could slip her cuffs. He's driving down the road and he notices that people are passing him and waving their arms. He looks in his outside mirror and sees a bra being pushed through the open window. In his rear-view mirror he sees Shara with her feet in the air and she's taking off her panties. She's as naked as a Jay Bird. He hurries and runs the windows up and calls in to have a female officer with a blanket meet him at booking." There again is laughter but not because of the actions of Shara but imagining what deputy Morris must have been thinking. Kevin flipped a page in his note book and continued.

"Then there was a sad case that took us quite a while to process. We received a call from the Quality Inn downtown alerting us to a possible death in their Bridal Suite. I took the call since all deputies on shift were tied up. When I arrived the night manager took me to the area and the door to the suite was locked, but we could hear someone moaning and sobbing. I pressed my ear against the door, and I heard the person sobbing and saying, *I'm sorry, Oh I'm so* sorry, and then gut-wrenching sobbing. The manager called out that he was there, and the sobbing subsided. I heard the latches and lock being messed with and then the door opened. There stood a young man, I found out later that he was twenty-seven years old, he was in his boxer shorts only, his face was red as a beet and over his shoulder I could see the body of a female, partially covered lying on a bed. The guy walked away and sat on the bed next to the female and through his sobs and his hands that covered his face he said:

"She's dead! Oh my God, she's dead," and the sobs continued. I checked the body for any signs of life, there was none, and the body was cold. I then raised the sheet that was covering her to see if there was any signs of trauma, there was none that I could immediately see, so I covered her completely and turned to the young man.

"What happened?" I asked. He didn't answer so I asked again "What happened here?" I got no response. It was obvious that he had been drinking a lot. After calling for the coroner I took the man, his name I learned later to be josh, I took him in custody and took him from the scene. I put him in my patrol car. Then I went back in and took pictures of what appeared to be a crime scene…

Josh Payton met and married Darlene Cataline when he was twenty-two years old, and she was twenty. They were a perfect match for each other. Over the few years of their marriage they had maintained an almost unhealthy sex life. They engaged one another before sleeping at night, when waking in the morning and any other time that they could sneak away to some secluded spot. Both worked as technicians at the hospital and when they passed in the passage ways it was not unusual for one or the other to grab and pull a willing participant into an empty stairway or an unused office or lab, and love on each other for a few moments.

They had celebrated each of their anniversaries, but one, by getting away to some hotel or motel for a weekend. Both Josh and Darlene liked drinking wine, so these always get included at romantic dinners, lots of wines and expensive champagne. The one anniversary they missed was when their daughter Mildred was too young to be left with his or her parents. She was three now and she enjoyed spending time with the Grannies. On this occasion she was with Darlene's parents.

After returning from a private candle light dinner Josh and Darlene decided to relax a bit and watch a movie. As usual they couldn't keep their hands off each other and began to engage in some casual foreplay. All of a sudden, Darlene seemed to be in some distress, but in his level of inebriation he failed to recognize it as such and continued to hold her head…..

"It took quite a while for the coroner to arrive," Kevin was continuing the story. "After getting all the information about how things went down I was really concerned about the guy, so after the body was removed I decided to hold him for his own protection. He's now on suicide watch. All the details regarding the situation are in my report. I expect to get a cause of death report sometime today and proceed from there."

"Was the next of kin notified," Steve asked.

"The coroner is handling all of that," Kevin said. "I assume he did that this morning after talking with the girl's husband. All the contact information of both families is in my report should this turn into a full-blown criminal investigation."

"Keep me updated on this thing," Steve said to Kevin. "How did you fare under the full moon George?"

"Nothing as exciting as Kevin's evening," George said. "My team and I did manage to bring the runaway and extortion case to a close of sorts. Based on the information that Sheriff Spence provided us we apprehended the fella, Bart Manning, that tried to extort the Parson family, and we found the runaway, Daniel Parson, at the residence occupied by Mr. Manning. We're holding Manning pending charges being filed by the State of Texas and the boy is currently detained prior to Child Protective Services taking charge of him. I'll have a full report on your desk as soon as all contacts have been made. The kid does not want to go home. It'll be interesting to see how the two agencies, Texas Family Protection and our Child Protectives services handle it."

"If I were to chance a guess," Steve surmised. "That young man is going to be bounced around in the systems for some time. Well, I have nothing pending this morning so let's get caught up on all the paper work so that I'll be prepared when the media starts calling and wanting answers. Let's hit it."

About mid-morning Kevin got a call from the coroner's office. The autopsy had been completed and the cause of death determined to be Dysphagia.

"You're gonna have to put that in English for me sir," Kevin said.

"Dysphagia," Dr. Perkins re-stated. "It' spelled D-y-s-p-h-a-g-i-a but pronounced Dis-FAY-juh, spelled D-i-s -f-a-y-j-u-h. Have you ever drank something or while eating, what you were eating or drinking went down the wrong way?

"Yes sir, many times." Kevin responded.

"Well", Dr. Perkins continued. "Swallowing is a complicated process, but to put it simply, liquid or food that we swallow sometimes ends up entering our wind pipe, called the trachea instead of the esophagus. This causes coughing reflexes or gagging. If whatever is in there isn't expelled it causes real problems, a person can expire."

"I understand, sir," Kevin said. "But there was no indication that the lady was eating or drinking anything,"

"When you processed the room, did you by chance see any kind of lubricating substance around?" The Dr. asked.

"I picked up the pictures I took from our photo lab earlier, let me see." Kevin dumped an envelope containing the processed film and the photos on his desk and spread the photos out. There on the night stand beside the bed was a wallet, a set of keys and a tube. Kevin could make out the writing on the tube It said L-Arginine. "Yes sir, there is a tube of L-arginine on the night stand."

"That confirms what we found logged in the trachea of the deceased," the Dr. said. "We also found semen on the tongue and in the back of the throat. It can be deduced that the deceased was engaged in oral sex. There are indications that there had been sexual intercourse activity, and a portion of lubricating gel became logged in the trachea. This death did not happen through natural causes, it's definitely a homicide."

Steve and Mertle stopped over at the Manor to have lunch with Craig and Martha. Once everyone was settled at the table, Steve made it a point to thank Craig for his help with the Bart Manning situation.

"The kid, Daniel Parsons, definitely does not want to go home, Steve advised. "Things must be pretty bad there."

"Where is he now?" Craig asked.

"He's being held while CPS can process things with the Texas people," Steve said.

"What about the girls," Martha wanted to know.

"To my knowledge they're in the hands of Texas Family protective services," Steve advised.

"I heard on the news this morning that there was a suspicious death at the Quality Inn," Craig stated. "What's with that?"

"Yeh," Steve affirmed. "Normally the Green River PD would take a call in that area, but they were swamped just like us. When dispatch called for an available unit Kevin took the call. He never in his career ever gone on a case like it."

"Well are you going to keep us in suspense?" Mertel asked. "Come on, tell us about it."

"A couple were celebrating their marriage anniversary and were making love when the wife expired," Steve tried to explain.

"Wow!" Mertel exclaimed. "What a way to go."

"Not really," Steve countered. "She choked to death."

"Eeeeew," Mertel reacted. "Not a good way to go."

"So what happens to the husband now?" Martha asked.

"The coroner has deemed the death a homicide. Because of the husband's actions and or inactions, he's being charged with involuntary manslaughter," Steve said.

"What a tragic end to two lives," Martha mused. Everyone was quiet for some time, all deep in their own thoughts. Then Martha spoke again,

"By the way," she began. "While you guys were playing cops and robbers the other day, there was a call from an old associate of yours, Matt Kessler. I forgot to tell you."

"Matt Kessler!" Craig exclaimed. "By golly, What did he say?"

"When you get a chance give him a call," Martha said. "the number is taped on the phone."…..

CHAPTER 8

After a change in City Council members, whose decisions were not favorable to the needs of the Rock Springs police Department, Matt Kessler and Pappy Masters, his chief of Detectives retired. The old Martenson Ranch out in the Wind Rivers had been put up for sale and the two of them bought it. They remodeled the main house and built a thirty-foot-high platform that they put a twenty-six-hundred-gallon water tank on. They turned the bunk houses into sleep rooms and made them available to hunters, hikers and people doing research or geological studies in the Wind Rivers Range. Modernized the old barn and bought a dozen trail horses. Wox and Little Owl, the Native American couple that had taken care of the place for Peggy Mortenson, were kept on as care takers and doubled as guides....

Back at the apartment, Craig immediately dialed the number that Martha had taped to the phone. The phone rang several times before a machine picked up the call.

"White River Ranch Guide Services," the message began. *" This is Matt Kessler, probably out n about. Please leave your name and number, a short message and I'll return your call. Thanks for calling."* There was a beep and Craig spoke up.

"A blast from the past you ole geezer," he said. "Craig Spence here. What the hell have you done? Where are you? I'll be around all day. Give me a call."

While he waited, Craig watched a national news cast on the TV. He watched a live viewing of President Reagan and Gorbachev giving a news conference in Washington D.C. at the white House and he listened to commentators hyping the upcoming Super Bowl between the New York Giants and the Denver Broncos. The phone rang.

"Hello, Craig Spence here," he said.

" Good day Mr. Spence, My name is Dorothy Mosely, and I am with Texas Family Protective Services." Craig was a little disappointed, he had hoped it would be Matt.

"Yes Ms. Mosely," Craig responded. "What can I do for you?"

"It is my understanding, sir," Ms. Mosley began. "That you and members of your family were involved with a case that I have been assigned to investigate," Dorothy stated. "The investigation is regarding the welfare of Beth Ferguson and CeCe Parsons, two female juveniles that ran away from Sweetwater, Texas and were taken into custody in Sweetwater County, Wyoming; You are familiar with these persons, are you not?"

"I am, and I've been concerned about those kids," Craig responded. "How are they and where are they?"

"They are in the custody of Texas family Protective Services," Ms. Mosley advised. "We are about to wrap up our investigation regarding a disposition in their cases. The reason I've contacted you sir, is to determine if you may have some knowledge about the girls that we may not be privy to and perhaps might wish to make a recommendation in their regard."

"The youngsters weren't in our presence very long," Craig began. "We fed them and cleaned them up. I did have an opportunity to chat with them both. My guess is that the little red head, I think her name was CeCe, she really wanted to support her brother. The conditions for her in the home had no cause for her decision to run off. If I were in a position to decide her fate, I'd get her out of the system and back to home ASAP."

"I appreciate your input, sir," Ms. Mosley commented. "I will relay your recommendation in my final report. Do you have any input regarding Beth, the other juvenile?

"You know," Craig began. "When I talked with Beth, her explanation of her home life reminded me of the battered wife syndrome, except this is a case of the battered child. She deplores her situation but still loves her abuser. Beth has strong feelings for her parents. If there were some changes in the fathers behavior, she'd be very happy at home. I have no knowledge of her father of course, but I have a pretty good understanding about people. My gut tells me that that man loves his daughter but hasn't been able to express it. Again, I don't mean to tell you how to do your job, but if I was in a position to make the call, I'd put pressure on him. I'd return the girl back to the home with some serious conditions and direct supervision."

"You must have been a great dad to your daughter," Ms. Mosley said.

"You'd have to ask her about that," Craig responded.

"I did," Ms. Mosley revealed. "Her name and information was on the report I received from the Wyoming Child Protection people, and I called her. She's the one that recommended that I speak with you."

"Looks like you've been pretty thorough," Craig commented.

"I try to be sir, and I thank you for your time and insight," Ms. Mosley said. "I wish you a good day sir." With that she was gone. Craig sat for some time, just looking at the phone and hoping that in some small way he might have helped those kids.

Matt Kessler spent the entire day on a trail ride with a tourist group, into the depths of the scenic Wind Rivers. After seeing his charges off, watering, feeding and caring for the horses, it was late when he settled down for the evening and checked the messages on his phone. There were several regarding future trail rides and some from persons wishing to make arrangements for room accommodations and a smile crossed his face when he came to the message from Craig Spence. After first taking care of business he dialed Craig's Number, and Craig answered.

"Craig Spence here," he said.

"Hey you," Matt answered. "How the hell are ya?"

"Boy it's a good thing I don't have caller ID," Craig said. "I would probably hang up. Every time I ever got a call from you, it meant trouble." Both Chuckled. "What's this Wind River Ranch Stuff? What have you done?"

"I really wasn't ready to retire and kick back like you did," Matt replied. "The city sorta forced me into it. The Council decided to cut the department budget along with a few others In order to move funds to a recreational complex project. We were already struggling to maintain, so I decided I didn't need the aggravation anymore.. Pappy was fed up too, so we put our heads together, figured we could invest in something we'd like to do and jumped at an opportunity. The Old Mortenson ranch was up for sale at a fire sale price and the rest is history. How are things with you my friend?"

"Good," Craig responded. "I didn't do anything as grandiose as you, but I've kept myself busy making scenic post cards and a few posters. You might have seen them in the Merch down town in Green River and the Mall in Rock Springs."

"I have," Matt said. "That's one of the reasons I called you. Pappy and I have taken tons of pictures of scenic spots in this range, but we don't know how to market them. Nor do we really want to get involved in that part of the business. You already have a thing going. We'd like for you to take a look at our stuff and see what could be done, maybe some post cards could be made and used to advertise this place. What do ya think?"

"The last time we were together I bought lunch. Who does the cooking out there?" Craig asked.

"The wife of our caretaker couple does it, why?" Matt questioned.

"I'm inviting myself to a meal. That would be a good time to go over your stack of pictures."

"You're welcome whenever, but we just have raw film, no prints," Matt advised.

"We need to get that film developed before it gets damaged somehow. Tell ya what," Craig indicated he had an idea. "It's a great excuse for me to come out there, might even bring Martha for the ride. I'll pick up the film and have prints made. It'll cost ya dinner, deal?"

"Deal," Matt responded. We don't work on Monday's, that is we don't work with the public on Monday. That's the day we spend taking care of equipment, the horses and tender loving care stuff, including us. Come see us."

"It'll be good to see you again. Was there another reason for your call?" Craig asked.

"Oh- yeh," Matt remembered. "I'm still a member of the National Chiefs of Police Association. The Wyoming Attorney General contacted the Association regarding the formation of a Voluntary Commission to review complaints and law suits against law enforcement officers and departments and make recommendations regarding disposition of cases or changes in policies and procedures. They are considering the makeup of the Commission to include active enforcement people and members of the citizenry. I've considered throwing my name in the hat to be considered and I was wondering if you might be interested."

"Ya know, Matt," Craig began. "I think such a Commission is really a good idea, but I've made a commitment to Martha not to get too involved with such things anymore. I'm going to honor that commitment."

"I respect that Craig," Matt said. "There would be no exposure, and it is my understanding that the Commission would only meet when there was a case to review. There will be notification of all the particulars sent out to those who submit their names for consideration, can I submit your name so that you can receive the information?"

"Sure," Craig said. "It would be interesting to see what they have in mind, but I'm not committing to anything."

"Gotcha," Matt acknowledged. "Give me a call when you decide to come out, okay?"

"Will do," Craig replied. "Nice talking with you." The conversation with Matt ended there, but Martha had been listening.

"From your side of that conversation it sounded like Matt is trying to get you involved with something, What is it?" she asked. Craig explained what Matt had told him and what he had consented to.

"Be careful," Martha cautioned. "These thing have a tendency to morph into time consuming endeavors. I know you, and if there is a chance that you can, you will. You don't have to use me as an excuse if it's what you want to do, but let's see what it's all about."

CHAPTER 9

Daniel found himself in a confusing and stressful situation. When he first arrived back in Texas he was placed in a juvenile detention center. Rooms were like cells and the doors were always locked. There was a small glass window in the door so people could look in without opening it. The walls were bare, there were no windows, and the only light was inset in the ceiling and covered with a heavy wire mesh. There was a sink and a toilet in one corner of the room.

He had been detained for two days before anyone came to interview him. There were several other boys being detained there and twice a day he was let out of his room for an hour to participate in group activities. On the third day of his confinement he was taken to a conference room where two people were there to talk with him, one of whom was a psychologist and the other a representative of the Texas Family Protective Services.

During the interview, the psychologist immediately recognized that Daniel's behavior was symptomatic of a person with Autism Spectrum Disorder. He would not make eye contact, was mostly unresponsive when spoken to. When asked a question he flapped his hands as if to ward off having to answer. During the interview Daniel seemed to have difficulty paying attention to what was going on and looked away from the interviewers and made contortions with his mouth and face. The one thing that they were able to ascertain was that he did not want to go back to the home he had run away from. The Psychologist believed that the extreme conditions that Daniel had found himself in was aggravating his condition and recommended that he be moved to a foster home environment while his case was being processed.

Daniel was moved to the home of Sarahlee Higgins. Sarahlee was a petit woman with graying hair that she wore pinned on top of her head, twinkling grey eyes and an engaging smile. Her five- foot frame was a ball of energy. She had grown up on a farm where she learned to care for animals- pigs, sheep, goats, and horses. At the age of twenty-five she married a college professor, and they moved to Texas where he taught at the Community College in Sweetwater. They never had children, so after he died from a massive heart attack, she purchased a hundred and twenty acres outside the town, started an animal rescue operation and became a certified Foster Parent.

When Daniel was brought to her, she literally ran to him with her arms outstretched and pulled him to her with a hug. Not being used to such affection Daniel tried to pull away at first, but Sarahlee was persistent and continued to squeeze and even ruffled his hair.

"My," she said." What a handsome young man you are. Welcome to Sarahlee's Animal Rescue." Just as she was hugging Daniel, a fluffy calico cat was rubbing its self on the insides of his legs. Never having had a pet he stepped away. Sarahlee reached down and picked up the cat and handed it to Daniel.

"Here," she said. "This is Cassy. Hold her, she would love that." Daniel stiffly cradled the cat which climbed out of his grasp, climbed up on his shoulder and draped itself around his neck. Sarahlee took the cat.

"Come," she said taking Daniel's arm. "Let me show you where your room is, and I'll introduce you to the other children that live here."

The house was a long structure, one level with lots of windows and several entrances like a motel. As they walked across the yard to the house, they were followed by a gaggle of large white geese that honked at them as they followed. Daniel had never seen geese before, and he kept looking over his shoulder at them. Sarahlee assured him that they would not bother him and that they always honked at strangers. The geese weren't the only things that caught Daniels attention. There was a large three-legged dog that kept pace with them across the yard, several baby goats were romping on top of a pile of dirt near a fenced in yard where chickens were. Daniel had seen chickens before.

Sarahlee opened one of the doors to the house and guided Daniel inside. He stood in a small sitting room that had a couch, a small table with two chairs, a bean bag type chair and there was a window that looked out over the farm. Through the window Daniel saw some horses, donkeys and a strange animal that Daniel had never seen before, grazing out there. He pointed and turned to Sarahlee.

"What's them," he asked.

"Those are Alpacas," she replied. "In some countries they are used to carry stuff on their backs, and their wool is used to make sweaters, shirts and all kinds of clothes. While you're here you'll learn more about all the animals out there." Daniel moved to the next room and there was a bed, dresser, a chair and a closet to hang clothes in. A door beside the dresser opened into another room and there was a toilet, a sink and a shower.

"This is your new home, Daniel," Sarahlee said." Where are the rest of your clothes?"

"Got none," Daniel responded. "These is all I have. When I left home I didn't take anything. You're not going to make me go back there are you?" Daniel asked.

"I only know that you are going to be with me until things are worked out with your mom and dad. Let's go out and meet the boys and girls that stay here."

"How come you have so many animals?" Daniel asked.

"They are animals that other people didn't want, that were injured, and people brought them here for me to take care of, or people could not take care of them anymore," Sarahlee said. "I take them, if they are sick I get them healthy again and then put them up for adoption and people give them new homes. The boys and girls that live here with me help me care for them. You'll be able to help too."

"I'd like that," Daniel said as he showed some excitement by waving his arms back and forth, walking backwards and looking all around.

There was a red and white barn some distance from the house and Sarahlee took Daniel inside. There were two girls and a boy sitting in one of the stalls feeding two lambs. The boy had one lamb, and one girl had the other. The other girl had a bottle of milk in each hand feeding the lambs. They stopped and stood up when they saw Sarahlee and Daniel.

Tony, Margaret, Shannon," Sarahlee called them by name. "This is Daniel, and he will be living with us for a while." The two girls, Margaret and Shannon, came over and gave Daniel a hug and welcomed him. Tony moved over and took Daniels hand and shook it. They all looked to be around Daniels age.

"You want to feed the lambs?" Tony asked, and they all sat on the hayed floor, cuddling and feeding the lambs. Saralee quietly left them to it. She knew that they would make Daniel feel at home and she would see them all when they came to lunch. She went back to the house where she had a small store room. In it she had pants and shirts and brand- new boxer type underwear that people had donated from time to time. She took out some clothes that she thought would fit Daniel and took them to his room and laid them on his bed. She'd take the ones he was wearing and wash them so that he'd have a change.

Dorothy Mosely also had the Parsons case and CeCe had been at the group home a week before an interview could be conducted. When she was able to meet with CeCe, the girl was wearing a green outfit similar to hospital scrubs. Everyone at the group home wore similar outfits, but different colors. If you were a newbie, a person that had been in the home less than two weeks, green was the color worn. Persons who had been at the home two weeks but less than a month wore the color purple, and anyone who had been there more than a month wore red. The staff wore the same type outfits, but they were flowered and multi-colored.

"Hello young lady," Dorothy said as CeCe was let into the interview room. "That green uniform surely accents your red hair."

"Hi," CeCe responded. "these clothes are awful, but everybody wears them."

"They look really comfortable, are they?" Dorothy asked.

"I guess so," CeCe responded.

"I'm from the Texas protective Services Department," Dorothy began. "My job is to figure out why you ran away from home and to recommend actions that address circumstances and conditions that impact your welfare. You understand what I'm saying?"

"The other girls here say that you will put me in some other home," CeCe said, near tears. "I don't want to go to another home. I want to go back to my home."

"What the girls say is only partially true, CeCe," Dorothy said. "If I find that conditions at your home are such that your wellbeing is questionable and that those conditions would continue to be present if you were returned to your home, I would certainly recommend that you be removed from that situation. But, if that is not the case, I would do what every I can to see that you remain in the home. Why did you run away CeCe?"

"I didn't really run away from home," CeCe explained. "I left with my brother. He wanted to run away, and I went with him. Do you know where my brother is?"

"No, I don't have his case," Dorothy advised. "Tell me, CeCe, before you ran, how were things at home?"

"For me, good I guess," CeCe said.

"Were you abused in anyway?" Dorothy asked.

"No, my Mom never hit me like she did my brother," CeCe responded.

"Why did your mom hit your brother?" Dorothy was curious.

"Some people said that Daniel might be autistic and would act out and make my mom mad, and she would hit him," CeCe explained.

"Were these people doctors or psychiatrist?" Dorothy asked.

"I don't know what that is, but it was just some people in our church," CeCe revealed.

"What church do you go to," Dorothy probed. "Are you Catholic, Methodist, Baptist or some other church?"

"Faith Ministry is the name of the church.," CeCe responded. "My father is the preacher.

We all go to the church school and learn how to cook, sew, how to take care of money and other things that have to be done around the home. They call it home education."

"What about math and science, geography and history?" Dorothy wanted to know.

"I don't know about any of that. Maybe the upper grades. I don't know what they learn," CeCe said.

" Have you ever been to a public school?" Dorothy asked.

"No, but I'd like to," CeCe said. "Those kids have fun, and they play sports and stuff. We don't have any of that, and they wear nice clothes."

"What do you wear?" Dorothy wanted to know.

"Long ugly dresses," CeCe responded. Dorothy paused while she caught up with her note taking.

"How about after school? What do you do when you get home after being in school all day?" Dorothy wanted to cover all bases regarding CeCe's life experiences.

" Girls just help their mom's around the house and make sure dinner is ready for the men when they come in," CeCe recalled. "The boys do stuff that they learned in shop at the school, fix stuff or make new stuff."

"What about friends," Dorothy asked. "Do you have lots of friends?"

"I have one good friend," CeCe responded enthusiastically. "Beth, she was with us when we ran away. She's here too but I don't get to see her a whole lot. She wasn't treated very nice at home."

"What would you like to happen CeCe?" The question caught CeCe a little off guard, but she gathered herself quickly.

"I want to go home. I miss my Mom and I miss my brother. I'd like to go to a regular school and be like other kids. I'd like to learn some of that other stuff you talked about, Math and science, geography and stuff."

"You didn't say you missed your dad," Dorothy said. "Don't you miss him too?"

"I guess. He's really strict," CeCe said, a little forlorn. "He and the other men in our church don't think women and girls are as good as boys and men. But I guess I miss him too, not as much as my Mom."

It was a couple of days later that Dorothy Mosley met with Ken and Terresa at her office. Terresa came dressed in a very colorful Moo Moo type dress; her hair neatly styled to impress. Ken appeared in clothes that he would wear on his job, and with Bible in hand. Dorothy began by introducing herself and the purpose of the interview. She advised them that the interview was being recorded and received their consent. Then she got a surprise, Ken spoke up.

"Ms. Mosley, I can probably save us all a lot of time. I had to take time off from work to come to this meeting and I'd like to get back to it as soon as I can. Are you familiar with the parable in the bible, Luke 15:17 -20?"

"I'm not sure Mr. Parsons, Dorothy responded. "I understand that you are a minister, but we're not here today for a sermon, however, why don't you enlighten me."

"The parable relates to a father and his prodigal son. The son took his inheritance from his father and went off to live his life as he wished. When he had exhausted his means he returned to his father's house and his father accepted him without hesitation. That's very similar to this situation and I accept my daughter back without hesitation."

"Oh yes," Dorothy said. "I seem to recall that upon the sons return, the father accepted him and hired him on as one of his servants. The difference, as I understand the situation, is that CeCe was a servant before she ran off and I believe you have the wrong slant on this. You see what we're here to determine is if it is in her best interest to accept you back. I've visited with your daughter, a bright young lady, and she wants to come home. My job is to ascertain if her return to the home environment, that she sort to escape from, is in her best interest. My first question for you sir, is CeCe registered in a state accredited school?" The question stunned Ken, and he sat with his mouth open, hesitating to reply. Terresa spoke up.

"My husband has established a school within the church over which he presides."

"So, I ask you the same question Mrs. Parsons. Is CeCe registered in a state accredited school?"

"I'm not sure if our school is state accredited," Terresa said. "My husband took care of such matters. Ken, what's the answer?"

"It's a church school and we take responsibility for our children's education," Ken responded.

"So the answer is no," Dorothy stated. "Am I correct Mr. Parsons?"

"I suppose you are," Ken agreed. "Our children are taught in relation to our religious believes."

"It is not the policy of the Texas Family Protection agency to involve itself in the realm of a person's religion or their religious beliefs, unless the acts perpetrated through such beliefs jeopardize the wellbeing of a family member, in this case a child."

"We have never abused CeCe," Teresa said, tears beginning to stream down her face. "Please don't take our baby from us."

" I don't really need to continue this interview," Dorothy advised. "I have spoken with your daughter, and I know what her desires are. You have verified for me what the conditions at home are like. I don't usually do this but for the sake of everyone concerned I'm going to tell you what my recommendation to my superiors will be. One: That CeCe be tested to determine what her grade level is. Two: CeCe may be returned to the home under strict supervision and you, her parents, must register her in a state certified public or private school. I thank you for coming in and you will be notified by letter of the department's decision."

Dorothy Mosley also visited with Beth Ferguson. Her green outfit was not becoming. The bottoms were too big, and the top was difficult to keep on the shoulders. After Dorothy explained who she was and what the purpose of the interview was, she began questioning in a manner that would confirm information that she already had.

"Beth, did you attend school before you decided to join CeCe and her brother on their venture?"

"Yes," Beth responded. "We all attended our church school."

"What type of subjects were you taught in your school?" Dorothy wanted confirmation.

" We learned the basics," Beth began. "Reading, writing and arithmetic in the early grades. After I got into the fifth grade most of the stuff I learned was how to make and mend clothes, cooking and baking, handling money, it's about home finances and then we have bible studies."

"What grade are you in," Dorothy asked.

"I'm in the eighth grade," Beth replied. "Or at least I was. I don't know what will happen if I go back,"

"Do you want to go back?" Dorothy seized the opportunity.

"I miss my mom," Beth said. "I really miss her. I don't miss school it's no fun."

"What about your Dad," Dorothy probed.

"I don't miss him," Beth said. "He has always been very mean to me and my mom. I don't remember when he wasn't drinking and yelling at us."

"Did he ever hit you," This question was to confirm what Walt had alluded to when Dorothy interviewed him and Stella.

"That was the worst part," Beth revealed. "I never knew when I had done something that would set him off. Little things would upset him, and I'd be struck."

"Did your Dad ever hit your Mom?" Dorothy asked.

"Not that I ever saw," Beth replied. "He just yelled at her a lot."

"I guess you really dislike your Dad, huh?" Dorothy setting up her next question.

"Not really," Beth said. "I just wish I had a Dad like other kids, one that acted like he liked me and did stuff with me. He's my Dad. I don't dislike him I just wish he was different." Tears began to well up in Beths eyes.

"What if your Dad stopped drinking, do you think you would be happy at home?" Dorothy asked.

"That would be nice. I think so. I'd sure give it a try." Beth wiped her eyes and looked longingly at Dorothy. She began to think that a change could happen.

" I'm going to recommend that you be returned home, but with close monitoring of your situation. I'm also going to set conditions. Your Dad must enter a rehab program to help him deal with his drinking addiction and I'm going to recommend that you be registered into a public or private school. What do you think?"

"I like it," Beth said with a big smile. " Boy, some of the girls here had me convinced that I would have to live in a place like this until I turned eighteen. Thank you."

Craig and Martha made the trip out to the old Mortenson Ranch and though they had never been there before were amazed at its rustic appearance. A fence with wood slats forming an x pattern lined both sides of the road leading to the ranch proper, and then broke out and surrounded the compound. Matt and Pappy had preserved most of the old wood that remained on the structures and had sprayed a wood finish to the insides of the main house that gave the walls a pleasant glow. All the furniture in all of the rooms was western style.

The outbuildings, of which there were four, had been reconstructed, however. There was a workshop and equipment storage building; a long building which had served as a bunk house that had been restored to accommodate sleepovers or persons wanting extended stays; a barn that housed the horses and several Alpacas that were used to carry tents, food, cooking utensils and such on over-night trail rides and a two-bedroom house, its exterior constructed of what appeared to be river rocks, that the caretakers lived in.

As Craig had feared, a lot of the film that Matt had showed signs of having been scratched and some showed blemishes that was probably caused by dust or inadvertent exposer to light. Craig thought that some of the scenes were just the ticket for post cards. Craig decided that he would take a trip or two to the locations that had been photographed and see if he could recapture some of the images.

Craig decided to make a trek, with Matt, into the depths of the Wind Rivers in the middle of the week when all agencies would be operating just in case they had trouble.

The day before he was to leave, he sat down with Martha and spread a map of the Wind River Range on the kitchen table.

"This is going to be a two-day trip," Craig said. "I want you to know what we'll be up to."

"Who's we," Martha asked.

"Matt and me," Craig responded. "I'd never attempt a trip like this alone. Those mountains are beautiful, but they are also treacherous and will eat the unwise and unprepared intruders alive. I'll pick up Matt tomorrow morning at the ranch; we'll then take the jeep about three miles into the Range, to the end of the Wind River Ranch property. Matt has a satellite camp site there and he keeps a road grader and a three-quarter ton Dodge crew cab pickup with a blade on it. We'll put all of our gear in the pickup and take it the rest of the way in." Craig took his finger and pointed to areas on the map and drew an imaginary line.

"We're planning to go up Silas Canyon here, to Schiestler Peak, up Wind River peak, which is thirteen thousand feet, then down to Slinks Canyon and up to the Shoshone National Forest and the Wind River Indian Reservation. We'll have to use old seldom used vehicle tracks made by Forest Rangers and fire crews. We'll have to clear the way in most areas with the trucks blade in some cases and then hike to the points we want to photograph."

"Are you up to such a trek?" Martha asked.

"We'll just take our time," Craig said. "Matt won't need to be back at the ranch for a trail ride until next week so there's no hurry."

"Will you be able to communicate with anyone from up there?" Martha was concerned.

"Matt has radios that we can talk to Pappy down at the Ranch," Craig assured her. "The radios are line of sight though, so depending on where we would be located will affect reception. When we're high up we should be able to reach out to Pappy."

The following morning, with cameras and a thermos full of hot coffee that Martha had prepared in hand, Craig headed toward the Wind River Ranch.

CHAPTER 10

Daniel had been at the animal shelter with Sarahlee a month before the State Department of Family Protective services sent a counselor by to do an evaluation. She expressed her concerns about Daniel's behavior. He wasn't violent or abusive, but he was very moody and at times hard to communicate with. His attention span was not very long, and his mind seemed to wander a lot.

The Counselor was an older gentleman, who showed evidence of little physical activity, Sarahlee thought. He was somewhat chubby, with a belly that was extended. He had black hair with a silver streak right down the middle of his head. He also had a goatee that was mixed with more gray than black. The short walk from his car to the front room of the house where Sarahlee had her office, winded him and he flopped down in the chair in front of her desk heavily, struggling to catch his breath. Sarahlee brought him a glass of water and introduced herself.

"I'm Sarahlee Higgins, and I'm the certified Foster Care Giver here. When they called and said someone would be coming today I expected one of the regulars, don't recall seeing you before."

"My name is Dan Cranston, Sarahlee. Good to know ya," he said between a couple of deep breaths. "I am assigned to the Special Operations Section, and we deal with cases that need special attention." Dan stopped speaking, took a sip of water and then continued. "I am by profession a psychiatrist and I've been assigned the Daniel Parsons case. According to the paper work I've been given, we could possibly be dealing with a case of ASD as well as parental abuse. What can you tell me about Daniel?"

Sarahlee had removed a folder marked DANIEL PARSONS from a file in the lower right hand desk drawer and she began to read from notes, like a diary, that she had maintained over the days and weeks that Daniel had been with her. She related her concerns about his behavior and then explained how he responded to the animals.

"Daniel decided that he would like to take care of the Alpacas as his project around here," she said. "His first meeting with them, however, was not very pleasant for him. We have two Alpacas, Thelma the mother and Tess, a Cria or young one. Daniel approached Tess too fast, and she spit at him, catching him on the forehead right between the eyes. After I got him cleaned up and calmed down I explained to him that spiting was an Alpacas way of defending themselves and that Tess didn't know him and that he had approached her too fast. Tess had walked off a ways, so I took him by the hand and together we slowly went to her. She didn't spit and she even let him touch her. After a few days they were chasing each other. I showed him how to check her feet and care for her toe nails and sometimes he remembers to check between her toes to make sure nothing is stuck there."

"What about the other animals and the other wards in your care," Dan asked.

"He does not do well with dogs," Sarahlee advised. "We have a few that are very friendly. He hates being nuzzled or licked by them. He won't go near the horses. The other children get frustrated with him because he doesn't pay attention and can't complete a task before he's off to something else that's mostly unrelated. I've explained his situation to them, and they tolerate him."

"There's no specific medical test to determine the suspected disorder and symptoms or severity vary widely," Dan began. "Observation of a child's social interactions, communication skills and behavioral issues are important in determining what testing may be required to confirm a diagnosis. What do you know of his home environment? According to the report I have, the young man ran away from home and was finally recovered in Wyoming. Has he related anything regarding his reason for leaving the care of his parents?"

" When he first came here he asked if I was going to make him go back to his home," Sarahlee explained. "The impression I got was that he didn't want to go. That's as much as I know."

"Well," Dan said. " I guess it's time that I met this young man and had a conversation."

"He should be in his room," Sarahlee said. "Come, I'll take you there and introduce you."

When Daniel wasn't helping to care for the animals or at meals he spent much of his time in front of the window in his room watching the animals interact with each other. That's where he was when there was a knock on the door to his room.

"Daniel, it's Sarahlee." He heard her say. "you've got a visitor." He hurried to open the door and there stood Sarahlee and a man he had never seen before.

"Hi," Daniel said to Sarahlee. "you want to come in?"

"Yes," Sarahlee said. "This gentleman would like to talk to you. He's from the State Department of Family Protective Services. His name is Dan, almost like yours."

"Hello, young man," Dan Said. "I'm glad to meet you. I've heard a lot about you from Sarahlee and I wanted to meet you in person. I've been asked to assess your situation and see how we can help you. I've been told that you ran away from home. Can you tell me why?" Daniel turned away from Dan and looked out the window. He was also fiddling with the collar of his shirt. He didn't respond to Dan's inquiry as to why he had left home. Dan pursued.

"Daniel, It would really help if we could look at each other while we're talking," Dan said. " It will help us get a feel for each other and get to know one another better." Daniel turned to face Dan. He made contortions with his mouth and wringing his hands as Dan continued.

"I understand you had quite a trip. You know, I've never ridden on a train. I've always wanted to, just never got the chance. How was it?"

"Cold, dirty and I really got hungry," Daniel replied, Still fiddling with his clothes.

"When did you decide to go for a ride," Dan asked.

"The day before we left," Daniel answered.

"Who's we, Daniel?" The report Dan had never mentioned others.

"My sister CeCe and her friend ,Beth. I wish CeCe was here with me."

"Why did CeCe leave," Dan continued to pry.

"When I said I was goin ta run away," Daniel explained. " She said she'd go too. She always looks out for me. When she said she'd go, her friend said she'd go too." Daniel stopped making faces and fiddling.

"What made you decide to go, Daniel?" Dan asked.

"My mom always beat on me," Daniel said, raising his voice. "Always she beat on me. I never want to go back there. I like it here; can't I stay here?" Daniel started fiddling again and turned to look out the window.

" Look at me, Daniel," Dan said in a low voice. "I want to be sure you understand what I'm about to say." Daniel turned back but he appeared to be looking over Dans head. Dan continued.

"Sarahlee only gives people a place to live for a short time. In your case, you will live here until we, you and I, decide what would be best for you. It's obvious that you don't want to go back home, so that means I have a lot of work to do. I need to meet with your Mom and Dad and see if there is some way we can make your life at home better or if it would be best for you to live somewhere else, a foster home maybe. What about school, Daniel? Do you go to school?"

"Yeh," I go to my father's church school," Daniel said.

"What grade are you in," Dan asked.

"I don' know," Daniel replied and began to make faces again.

" How do you get along with your teachers," Dan asked.

"Not good," Daniel replied half smiling. "They always make me go to the study room."

"Would you go home if your mom understood you better and wouldn't beat on you?"

"I don't trust her. She's always mad at me," Daniel said raising his voice again.

"Do you think you could trust me, Daniel?" Dan asked. "If I were to tell you that your Mom wouldn't beat on you, would you believe me?"

"Why," Daniel asked. "You don' know my Mom."

"Not yet," Dan said. "But I'm going to. I'm on your side, Daniel. My job is to do what is best for you. We'll work our way through this together."

"Do you know where my sister CeCe is?

" Wasn't she on the train with you?" Dan asked.

"Yeh, but she and Beth got off because they were cold and hungry. I stayed on because I was scared," Daniel advised.

"I don't know where she is, but I promise," Dan said. " I'll find out and the next time we talk, I'll let you know, okay?"

"Okay," Daniel said and for the first time Daniel looked Dan straight in the eye. Sarahlee had sat quietly while Dan talked with

Daniel. Dan gave her a nod indicating that he was through, and she escorted him out to his car.

"What do you think," Sarahlee asked. "Do you think he'll be removed?"

" It is my opinion that the young man has some form of ASD," Dan began. "The symptoms are different in each case. I want to consult with my colleagues and arrange for him to be tested in order that a treatment can be recommended. Child Protective Services cannot remove a child from the home without a court order unless there is an immediate danger to the child's physical health or safety, or the child has been a victim of neglect, sexual abuse, or human trafficking. At this point I'm not sure that the situation warrants such action. Thanks for your help and I'm sure we'll speak again. Have a nice day." With that Dan entered his car and Saralee watched as he left the property and drove down the main road.

Walt and Stella Furguson were required to appear before a judge In their quest to keep custody of their daughter Beth. During the hearing Dorothy Mosely, representing Child Protective Services Division of the Texas Department of Family Protective Services and the Child Bethea Furguson, laid out the results of her investigation and provided the court with the Departments recommendations which included conditions for Beth to be returned to the custody of the parents.

During the interview with the Judge, Beth expressed a desire to return to the home under the conditions recommended by Ms. Mosley. Walt Furguson expressed remorse for his past behavior and agreed to the conditions proposed by the court and Stella assured the judge that Beth would have her support. A court order was issued to require compliance under the laws of Texas and Beth was returned to the custody of her parents.

During a court proceeding, Dorothy Mosley testified to the judge that the Department found no evidence that Celine Parsons, nick named CeCe, was in any danger as defined by Texas Law and should be returned to the custody of her parents. She did, however, address the educational situation that CeCe was subjected to.

"Your Honor," Dorothy had said. " The child in this case is required to attend a school that was established by her father who is a self-ordained minister. The school is not accredited by the state and its curriculum does not meet the educational standards of the state. This child is of an age at which she should be at a grade six level. While in the custody of the state she was tested, and the results show that she performs at a fourth-grade level. It is the recommendation of this agency that the parents be required to register the child in a private or public, state accredited school."

After much discussion regarding the church school with Ken and Terresa the Judge ordered that CeCe be released to their custody . He did not order that she be registered in an accredited school.

Mr. and Mrs. Parsons," the judge addressed CeCe's parents. "It is not the desire of this court to get involved in the way you practice your religion, unless those practices have a negative impact on the welfare of a child that has been brought to the attention of this court. While your religious practices do not appear to place Celine in danger, physically or emotionally, it is evident, however, that she is being denied an opportunity to receive a standardized education that would prepare her for the rigors of her future. I'm not going to order you to register Celine in a public or private school, but if you don't, I am ordering The Department of Child Protective Services to monitor her educational progress, to include testing as required-that you will have to pay for- to insure that she can perform at the expected grade level commensurate with her age. The Department will report their findings to this court and make recommendations for any further actions that may be necessary."

From the east end of the Wind River Ranch property the going got tuff. Craig had never been in the Wind River Range, so he didn't know what to expect. Most of the areas that Matt had taken photos of were easily reached by hiking or horse trails. Access by vehicle was along forest roads used by forest rangers and Park and Wildlife personnel. The tracks were unmaintained, over grown in places and rutted by the constant runoff from melting snow in the higher elevations. The Vehicle that Matt had selected for this trip, Four-wheel drive with its raised profile and oversized tires, was well suited for navigating small streams and bogs that presented themselves as they picked their way through dense wooded areas and open plateaus.

Craig was awed by the sheer beauty of the landscape. The immense rock formations, tall peaks and visons of the high country with its snow-covered vistas was breath taking. It made the slipping and sliding of the vehicle as it made its way through the bogs and bumping over rocky ledges almost unnoticeable. After a little over two hours they reached the first area that they wanted to photograph. the Schiestler Peak area. The peak is eleven thousand six hundred twenty-four feet high at its highest point and because of its altitude receives precipitation all year round, snow in the winter and thunderstorms in summer months.

The forest road ended at the eight-thousand-foot level and Matt and Craig had to hike down the mountain side, through stands of birch and undergrowth, to about the Seven-thousand-foot level to a plateau that overlooked the Sandy River basin. They stopped and sat up the camera equipment next to a natural spring that originated inside a slanted rock formation and flowed down the mountain side emptying into a small pool in the river below.

From their vantage point they could see the High Country Route that Matt had taken many tours into these mountains. In fact through his lens, Craig could see a group of hikers, all in a line moving along a ridge below the tree line on the peaks across from where they were positioned. They spent several hours photographing interesting scenic sites and eagles soaring above them against the sky.

When they decided to leave for the next site, turning the truck around was not an option. They would have to back out until they came to a spot wide enough to make the turn around. Craig walked behind the truck to give Matt a reference and keep the wheels in the tracks. It took a considerable amount of time before they found a spot and it was getting late, so they decided to spend the night there and head out at daybreak. It was also getting cool on that mountain. Matt had brought sleeping bags so after they had had sandwiches and pop they zipped themselves in the sleeping bags, Matt in the front seat and Craig in the back and called it a day.

In the wee hours of the morning they were awaken by a loud crack of thunder and the surrounding area was lit up by flashes of lightning followed by more thunder. The temperature had plummeted in the truck. It was raining and visibility through the trucks windshield was obscured. Craig looked out the rear side windows and when the lightning flashed he noticed that there was a mixture of rain and snow falling.

"It's a good thing we got this truck turned positioned in this spot," he said. "It's gonna be slick as snot when we drive out here at daylight."

"With the weather like it is we may not be able to get to the other sites," Matt observed. "It'll be best to use all the daylight getting down off this peak."

"Well," Craig said. "No use fretting about it tonight. Let's see if we can at least get some rest and we'll tackle whatever in the morning."

When morning came, Matt stepped out of the truck into two inches of wet snow. Visibility was severely restricted. He figured that a cloud bank was probably engulfing the peak. He noticed another condition that troubled him. The snow had made it very difficult to see where the vehicle tracks were that they had followed to this part of the peak. When Craig joined him outside the truck they tried to assess their predicament.

"Looks like we're stuck here for a while," Matt said.

"This fog is sure thick," Craig said.

"One man's cloud is another man's fog," Matt replied. "I think the peak is shrouded in a cloud. I can hardly see where the vehicle track is. We're stuck here until this stuff lifts."

It was several hours before the sun penetrated the cloud and the visibility improved to the point that the two could see a considerable distance. They decided to try and make their way down the mountain identifying the vehicle traveled area as best they could. As they moved through an area of standing pines, a stream cut across their path. When they had come up the hill this stream only had a couple of inches of water flowing down the hill. Now it was a torrent spilling out of it banks and Matt couldn't tell how deep it was. Considering the extra height of the truck's undercarriage and the size of the tires, Matt decided to put the truck through the stream.

The water had cut the banks of the stream quite deep and when the front wheels went over, the soil gave way, and the front wheels of the truck slid in the direction that the water was flowing. Using the four-wheel capability the truck made it to the other side of the stream easily, but the bank had been cut deep and the wheels just kept collapsing the bank, not able to climb over and finally just started digging themselves deeper into the soft soil and mud.

The water was just below their knees and freezing cold as Matt and Craig crossed to the other side to survey their situation.

"We're not gonna be able to drive out of here," Craig said. "Unless we can find some rocks or some wood to put under the wheels."

"I think that dirt will just keep falling away and we'd dig us in deeper. We'd freeze trying to get it done," Matt surmised. "I've got a better idea. This truck has a heavy-duty winch on the front." Matt began looking around and up ahead in the direction they wished to travel. He pointed in that direction. "Up ahead, see that pine tree about twenty yards or so? I'm going to loosen the cable on the winch and if you would walk it over there and wrap it around that tree, I'll use the winch to drag the truck's front end to solid ground and up out of there."

Craig took the hook at the end of the winch cable and slowly stretched the cable to the tree. Once he had the cable securely around the tree Matt activated the winch and the truck slowly began to cut through the soft soil and ended up on solid ground. Matt continued to use the winch until the truck was out of the stream.

Once out, Matt drove the truck forward until he came to an open area where they could take full advantage of the sun.

"Let's get out of these wet clothes," Matt suggested. "We can stretch them out over the trucks hood, and we'll get the heat from the engine plus the sun." They stripped off their shoes, socks and pants and did as Matt had suggested. They returned to the warmth of the truck's cab while the cloths dried. Then Craig groaned.

"Boy, I've got a really bad pain in my arm," he said, as they got comfortable. A short time afterwards Craig began to have difficulty breathing and there was a tightness in his chest. "Matt," he said. "I think I'm having a heart attack." Without a word Matt exited the truck and threw on his clothes. He just threw Craigs cloths on the back seat and as fast as was safe, drove the truck toward the main access road. He took a radio out of the trucks console and tried to contact Pappy at the ranch. The radio was line of sight and because there were still some peaks and ridges between them and the ranch he had to try several times as he headed out. Finally, he made contact.

"Yeh, Matt," Pappy responded.

"Get ahold of the Fire Department in Farson and have them meet me at the southwest entrance to the Wind Rivers," he transmitted. "I'm about twenty minutes from the entrance. Craig may be having a heart attack!"

The access road finally became less bumpy, and Matt was able to increase speed. The road slopped downward and in the distance Matt could see the main highway. He knew that time was of the essence, but it seemed that the time it was taking to get to the highway was in slow motion. Then his spirits jumped as he saw the red and blue lights flashing as an emergency vehicle was approaching the junction and closure was momentary.

"Hang tight, ole buddy," Matt said to Craig. "We're gonna get ya some help." There was no response.

The sun shining through the bedroom window had waken Martha. She had no plans for the day, so she had slept in. She would have stayed in bed a little longer, but the doorbell rang. Begrudgingly, she put on a robe, stepped into her slippers and went to the door. She looked through the peep hole but could see no one.

"Who's there," she asked. There was no answer. She opened the door just enough so she could see out and there was no one there. There was, however, a newspaper on the floor. *How nice,* she thought. She took the paper to the kitchen table, proceeded to pour a cup of coffee from the pot that had been prepared night before, set on a timer and automatically brewed coffee in the morning.

It was while she was sipping her coffee and perusing the paper that the phone rang.

"Hello, this is Mrs. Spence, can I help you?" it was Matt.

"Sit down, Martha, I've got some bad news for you," he said. She sat on the bench that was always at the table were the phone was.

"Good Lord, Matt what's wrong," she asked. Her heart was pounding in her chest.

"Craig had a heart attack," Matt told her.

"Oh, Merciful God! How is he? Where is he?" She had a lump in her throat and could hardly speak.

" An ambulance crew out of Farson got him stabilized," Matt told her. He's on his way to Casper by chopper. He was awake and talking when he left. He said to me "Call Martha, tell her I love her."

THE END

List of Characters

Craig Spence	Retired Sheriff of Sweetwater County
Martha Spence	Wife of Craig Spence
Katie	Daughter of Martha and Craig
Mertle	Martha's Friend
Steve Lolly	Sheriff of Sweetwater County
Kevin	Chief Deputy Sweetwater County
George Stenson	Chief Detective Sweetwater County Sheriff's Office
Tera Mosby	Jail Administrator Sweetwater County Sheriff's Office
Parker	Deputy Sheriff
Morris	Deputy Sheriff
Kennesy	Sweetwater, TX Police Officer
Dr. Perkins	Coroner
Tony Ward	Paty Thortons Attorney
Heather	Office Assistant to Sheriff Lolly
Milly	Sheriff Lolly's younger Daughter
Marla	Sheriff Lolly's oldest Daughter
Carolyn	Wyoming Child Protective Services Counselor
Dorothy Mosely	Texas Child Protective Services Counselor
Paul Thorton	Local Dentist
Paty Thorton	Wife of Paul Thorton
Sharon Thorton	Paul and Pat Thorton's Daughter
Molly Preston	Mother of Paul Thorton
Walt Ferguson	Energy Employee
Stella Ferguson	Wife of Walt Ferguson and Beth Fergusons Mother

Bethea (Beth) Ferguson	Daughter of Walt and Stella
Ken Parsons	Faith Ministries Minister
Terresa Parsons	Wife of Ken and Mother of Daniel and CECE
Daniel Parsons	Son of Ken and Terresa
Celine (CeCe) Parsons	Daughter of Ken and Terresa
Roberta Fairly	Colleague of Paul Thorton's
Marcy	Beth's bunk mate
Marline	CeCe's Bunk mate
Shara Smith	Drunk Lady
Josh & Darlene Payton	Husband & Wife celebrating their anniversary
Tobriena (Tony)	Owner of the Dusty Trail Café'
Bart Manning	Black Butt employee